The Mark of Trask

Michael D. George

A Black Horse Western

ROBERT HALE · LONDON

© Michael D. George 2011
First published in Great Britain 2011

ISBN 978-0-7090-9210-0

Robert Hale Limited
Clerkenwell House
Clerkenwell Green
London EC1R 0HT

www.halebooks.com

Typeset by
Derek Doyle & Associates, Shaw Heath
Printed and bound in Great Britain by
CPI Antony Rowe, Chippenham and Eastbourne

Dedicated to Doc Bunston. Thanks, pard.

PROLOGUE

There were many in the wilds of the West who became legends for little more than being ruthless killers. Men without souls who just happened to be fast with their chosen weapons. Men who killed the way decent folks breathed – without thought or remorse. Then there were those who achieved greatness and immortality due to their bravery or flamboyant deeds. Some found fame due to the insatiable appetite of the folks in the east who read about their exploits in dime novels. Few ever discovered if their heroes were as brave as the tall tales claimed them to be. Even fewer really cared. For the truth was no substitute for a good story.

Then there was the small handful of legendary figures who did not fit into any of the above categories. Men who simply existed and roamed the wild lands like knights from ancient times. Men who shunned publicity of any kind and yet became legends to equal all other varieties. Men who were willing to act as champions for the weak or oppressed for little more than a simple touch of a wide hat brim and a smile.

Legends that still haunt our distant and collective memories have become engraved into our very souls. Names once heard which become unforgettable still linger in our present day literature and colour our own mundane lives.

Then there was the man known as Trask.

A man alone. A true legend by any yardstick.

Yet Trask was unlike any other man who ever rode the West in search of the one thing all men seek. The place where he might find the answers to the questions which burned into his every sinew. The place where the truth reigned.

Yet who actually was Trask?

Few ever got to know the rider who owned the handsome pair of Eagle-Butt Peacemakers with their unique mother-of-pearl grips showing an eagle attacking a rattler. Even fewer would have believed one word of the story which had haunted the lone rider for decades.

Only the man branded by the name upon the hand-tooled gunbelt actually knew what his true name was. Yet since the day he had first purchased the beautiful yet deadly guns he had become known as TRASK. The name branded into the leather belt between two lines of bullets.

No one had ever called him anything else from that fateful time on. It was as though his own humanity had become part of something else. He had become Trask.

But time had travelled on just as he had himself. Now he was no longer young but feeling the cold winter of his days approaching fast.

The man had become a legend. Or more accurately it had been the guns which were famed.

The guns of Trask.

Guns which never failed to clear their holsters whenever the man was in danger. Guns which never missed their targets even when the man himself seemed to be doomed. Guns which always found his hands as though guided by some unknown or unseen power he himself was oblivious of.

Whoever the man who was known as Trask had once been, he knew that he would always be Trask to all who set eyes upon the deadly weapons he travelled with.

He knew that not even death would end the legend of Trask. For the man who did not consider himself as the owner of the strange guns but merely their present caretaker, believed they would find another possessor as soon as he himself died. There would be another Trask, another pitiful creature like himself who would become enslaved to the handsome weaponry; become their servant but never their master.

Yet death did not come easily to anyone who wore the gunbelt with the name of Trask emblazoned upon its still pristine leatherwork.

The man had long believed that the guns protected their owner. They would not allow anyone to outdraw him; never fail to kill those who tried to kill him.

If death were to catch up with Trask it would have to do so naturally. It would have to creep up on him during the night like a ravenous cougar. Catch him with his guard down. Or perhaps it was simply a matter of time. Death never played favourites. The Grim Reaper would have his chosen prey when the sand in the hour glass finally ran out. Even the guns could not stop age from claiming him when it was time to die.

Or could they?

Legends never truly die.

At least, not when they are wearing the guns of Trask.

ONE

There was a long wide valley far below the high trail which straddled the misty tree-covered mountain. It was as close to heaven as most men would ever get and yet those who usually rode its narrow perilous route were the kind which would never find themselves invited within a million miles of anywhere quite so hallowed. This was a trail mostly frequented by the worst breed of two-legged vermin. Men who sought refuge in the high country far beyond the eyes of those who might recognize them.

But the horseman who had steered his resolute chestnut stallion to this place was not of their kind. He was a very different type of visitor to this remote land. A stranger who travelled this path for no better reason than it had been there before him. Most men would have been afraid of the sheer drop beside the hoofs of his mount but not

Trask. Trask trusted the horse beneath him more than he had ever trusted any man. The horse had never let him down. Never betrayed him. No man had ever earned that kind of trust.

It was a stunning vista which greeted Trask's tired eyes as the stallion proceeded on and on up the dusty golden path beside and above countless straight trunked trees.

The silver haired horseman reined in and studied it. He felt no emotion. All emotion had long since left his soul as he had vainly searched for a place where he might belong. Yet for all his questing he had never even come close to locating anything except trouble.

Trask held the reins in his gloved hands and stared down at the land as the morning sun began to spread across it. It was like watching a painter instantly creating a masterpiece yet he still felt nothing. Nothing except a despair which had haunted him for the previous few months. He rubbed his flat belly and tried to make the constant ache go away but it remained. It was a strange feeling. A feeling of being both empty and full at the same time.

The rider was not old but time had taken its toll. His face was scarred by it. The cold and the heat of countless thousands of days of constant travelling through the vast land he had once relished, had made him old. Trask knew there was nothing anyone could ever do to stop the progress of time, for all living creatures were the victims of the same unseen enemy. An enemy far more lethal than any weapon the most savage of warlords could have ever envisaged. The passage of time and its brutal reality could never be defeated.

Some had only a little time whilst others were granted more but none of the living creatures who lived could last longer than their designated time. All living things were helpless to do anything but accept the cards they had been dealt and play them to the best of their ability.

Trask gave a long sigh and looked down at the gunbelt hanging over the neck of his horse. The name TRASK stared back up at him as it had done for decades. His gloved fingers touched the black letters and felt the impression the branding irons had left long before he had first set eyes upon this hand crafted leatherwork. Then he looked at the pearl handled gun grips jutting up from each holster. A sense of fear washed over him.

Even after all these long years it was still the same. The same feeling of trepidation whenever he cast his eyes upon the matched Peacemakers.

'Reckon we oughta have us a little rest, Smoke, boy.' Trask went to ease himself off the saddle when he heard something echoing around the trees. He instinctively gripped the reins tightly and listened again. The sound had been muffled and taunted his ears. He wanted to swing the stallion around to get a better view of the land around him to see if he might get a clue to where the noise had emanated from but this was no trail to do anything except continue on in a straight line. There was no room for turning up here, he silently told himself.

Trask leaned back and squinted down over the tops of dark green trees. Whatever was down there in the valley, he could not see it. There might be a sprawling city for all he knew. Whatever lay beyond the trees, it was well hidden from the prying eyes of onlookers.

Then he heard the same sound.

A sound which was stifled somehow.

It was coming from beyond his high vantage point. Whatever it was that had made the noise, it had come from far down in the valley. Trask managed to stand in his stirrups and raised a gloved hand to shield his eyes from the low rising sun. He could not see anything. There was not even a hint of there even being another living crea-ture within a hundred miles of the place where he and his horse rested but he knew there had to be. For something had made the confounding noise.

Carefully Trask lowered himself down on to his saddle once more. He heard the noise again. This time it appeared to be further away. He shook his head. He knew all too well that sound had a habit of bending when there were enough sturdy trees in the way. Was that it? Were his faculties being ridiculed because of the unending forest?

This was a puzzle and Trask detested puzzles.

Puzzles were usually created by men to taunt other men. Sometimes nature threw one at the unsuspecting just to add to the confusion. Being a man who always had to discover the answers to all mysteries, Trask had to find out the answers to all riddles including this one.

Trask patted the neck of the horse. 'You as curious as me, Smoke, boy?'

The stallion snorted.

Trask bit his lower lip and tasted the whiskers which he knew should have been shaved away days earlier. The baffling noises were coming from down there, he told himself. Down there amid the trees.

The countless damn trees.

Again he heard it.

'Gunfire.' Trask muttered to himself firmly. 'I'm betting on that being gunfire. If'n it is, someone might be in trouble. Ain't but one way to find out.'

As though inspired, Trask leaned over the neck of his horse and the infamous gunbelt and slapped the long ends of his reins at the stallion's tail. The horse responded as it always did and began to make pace up the narrow trail.

'C'mon, boy.' Trask heard himself calling out as though he were young once again. 'Let's go find out who the hell is shooting and why.'

The stallion and its master thundered fearlessly along the trail which was little wider than the horse itself. Higher and higher they climbed. Trask ducked low branches with the ease he had once taken for granted; the fiery stallion never put a foot wrong. The horseman was alive again: all his misery seemed to have evaporated in the dust which trailed them.

Every long stride of the chestnut seemed to be taking them both back to earlier days. Days when there was nothing but life ahead of them. Taking them away from the reality that most of their days were now behind them both.

The stallion thundered up the twisting trail. All obstacles either side stepped or jumped. The handsome stallion leapt as though it were a two-year-old and its master a mere youngster upon its wide back.

For a quarter of a mile the pair had travelled upward and then the trail started to slope down. Now they were heading in the right direction, Trask thought. Now they were heading down to where the mystery dwelled; to where the answers to the puzzle might be located.

Tree trunks and a twisting overgrown route did not slow their pace. They were now as one. Horse and master moving as though they had become the same gallant creature.

Trask found himself sucking in the fresh air like a drunkard swallows hard liquor. With ease and relish.

'C'mon, Smoke, boy.' He yelled out as he steered the horse with an expertise few others would ever achieve.

The stallion responded.

TWO

For the first time since man had initially ventured into the fertile valley the sound of ferocious gunfire filled its usually tranquil air and echoed around its vastness. For civilization had found another Eden in which to vent its wrath and soil its purity. There was little worse than those who existed by robbing and killing the innocent and the five outlaws who had discovered Mohawk Valley were in their element: they had found a pot of gold without even following a rainbow to its source. There were ranches along the length of the green valley and several small towns all connected together like the links on a chain. Evidence of hard work and an abundance of natural resources seemed to drip from every tree branch. The unscrupulous strong knew that this was a place where the weak would offer little or no resistance to whatever savagery they dished out. For it takes practice to become heartless and cruel and the citizens of Mohawk Valley had never been required to develop those unholy characteristics.

Until now the brutality of the outside world had never entered the valley. Until, that is, the gunfire had started to erupt from the barrels of the outlaws' six-shooters.

At the head of the small troop of wanted riders, 48-year-old Grant Largo led his venomous gang with both guns blazing as was his ritual. He led and they trailed behind. The four horsemen who ate his dust were all at least ten years younger than the notorious Largo.

Pete Tracy was a man who was more used to handling dynamite than his guns, but he always showed willing. Always to Tracy's right rode Snipe O'Mara, an outlaw who had earned his name during the war when his expertise at killing from long range had proven invaluable even though he had been on the losing side.

A few paces behind Tracy and Snipe riding drag was the youngest of them all, his only assertion to be with them at all was that he was Grant Largo's brother. Vance Largo was little more than a two-legged ferocious animal who lived for the thrill killing gave him. Even though he was only with them to make up the numbers, Vance was dangerous as all men with half a brain tend to be. To Grant Largo's left rode a man so dirty that he looked as though he had been painted in black tar. He gleamed from head to toe in untold years of grime. No skunk could have equalled his acrid aroma but no one had ever mentioned this to him and lived. He answered only to the name of Keets and was the fastest gunman of them all. His place in the gang was secured by his ability to dish out death whenever required. As they rode, Keets never once fired his arsenal of weaponry like the others. He rode and waited until he could draw and kill his prey within spitting distance. Not through any sense of the unwritten gunfighting code, but simply because he liked to see the destruction his bullets inflicted on his targets.

The trail through the very middle of the valley was well used and devoid of grass. Only dry sun-baked dust marked the route from one town to the next. Dust which spiralled heavenward from the wheels of the stagecoach as its driver used his hefty reins to whip the backs of his six horse team in a bid to escape the outlaws behind them.

The guard had placed himself upon the centre of the coach roof between an array of bags and unleashed his desperate retaliation from the twin barrelled scattergun whenever he managed to catch a fleeting glimpse of their pursuers through the choking plumes of yellow dust.

Yet the outlaws knew how to stay just beyond the range of the guard's mighty gun whilst still managing to hit their target with an ease only seven inch barrelled .45s could offer accurately.

Chunks of splintered wood kicked up into the face of the guard as he fired both barrels again and again. The stagecoach was becoming riddled with the bullets of the five riders who chased them.

'Can't ya get this thing moving any faster, Hoyt?' the guard screamed out, as his fingers fumbled in his pockets for more shells to load his smoking weapon with. 'We're sitting targets to them *hombres.*'

The driver was practically standing in the box as his hands and arms lashed the six lines of long leathers across the backs of the thundering team. But the burden of pulling the stagecoach and its human cargo had already begun to slow their feverish pace. Even lathered up the team could not respond to the driver's dire urgency.

'Can't ya kill the varmints, Snub?' the driver yelled back over his shoulder. 'Kill them before they kill us?'

'They got me pinned down here, Hoyt,' Parsons shouted back before taking aim once again. 'This damn gun ain't got the distance to kill any of them.'

'Then why don't ya use the Winchester, ya damn fool?' Hoyt called out. 'Scatterguns ain't no good at all unless folks is real close.'

Snub Parsons blinked hard and turned his head.

He looked at the wide back of his companion and gave a nod to himself. 'Damn it all. I done plumb forgot all about the repeating rifle. It's down by the strongbox. That's where it is.'

The stagecoach navigated around a sturdy oak with barely two of its wheels still on the ground. The driver whipped his team again as Parsons turned and crawled back toward him. Another flurry of bullets passed over Parson's head. He looped his legs out and then slid down into the box beside Hoyt.

'What kinda damn guard are ya anyways?' the driver snarled as he felt the heat of more lead fly to either side of him. 'I thought ya was experienced.'

'Shut the hell up, Hoyt. Ain't my fault someone's decided to try and rob us after all these years.' Parsons bent down and hauled the strong-box to one side and found the rifle. He remained in the box, pushed its knuckle guard down and then pulled it back up. A spent casing flew over his shoulder. 'Now I'll show them who got the range. Now I'll pluck me some turkey.'

The stage continued to thunder on along the trail at a speed neither of the Overland stage crew would ever have willingly chosen. Dust was covering both men in the driver's box as Parsons leaned over the seat and rested the long barrel of the Winchester on its metal luggage rail. The vehicle was bouncing like an ornery bronco as the guard closed one eye and tried to focus along the sights. The sound of panic stricken passengers screaming came from inside the coach as bullets tore into its fabric.

'Sounds like one of the passengers took a bullet. Can't ya keep this blasted thing from jumping up and down so much, Hoyt?' Parsons blazed out of the corner of his mouth. 'I'm trying to aim here, ya know.'

'Just fire the damn thing, Snub,' the sweat-soaked driver retorted loudly. 'Who knows, ya might get lucky and just hit one of them.'

Parsons was looking back into a cloud of dust – more dust than he had ever seen in his entire life. The hoofs of the six galloping horses were matching everything kicked up by the wheels of the stagecoach. Yet flashes of red venom were coming out of that wall of dust and hitting the fleeing stage. Splinters were showering over the guard as he licked the sights of the rifle in his hands.

He squeezed its trigger and sent a shot drilling into the dust which masked their attackers. They returned fire with a whole lot of interest. The guard blinked hard and glanced at his friend.

'Keep this crate even,' Parsons pleaded.

'I'm surely trying, Snub.' Hoyt spat, as his muscular arms fought to maintain control of the team who he knew were now blinded by terror. 'Can't ya shoot no faster?'

As though ridiculed into action, the guard did as Hoyt had requested. Five further shots followed from the Winchester in quick succession as Parson's index finger teased its trigger in between cranking the mechanism. Each bullet disappeared into the dust giving him no clue if he had managed to hit any of the riders who doggedly chased the coach.

Another volley of gunfire came back from the outlaws.

Before Parsons could prime the Winchester's magazine again he heard a sickening groan come from beside him. Hoyt arched and the reins fell from his powerful hands. A look of stunned shock carved across the driver's weathered features.

'I'm hit,' the driver croaked. 'I'm hit bad, Snub.'

'Hoyt?' Parsons released his grip on his rifle and grabbed at the torso of the wounded man. He eased Hoyt down. The driver slumped across the seat. Blood ran from his open mouth and a massive hole in his shirt front. 'Oh sweet Lord. You sure are hit, old timer.'

'Stop the coach. Them horses will run us into the gates of hell itself if'n ya don't stop them, Snub,' the driver managed to tell his companion, as his fingers clawed at the wooden board he lay upon. 'Stop them.'

Desperately Parsons turned and looked down at the tails of the two closest horses as they continued to gallop in blind panic. The guard leaned over. His arms stretched for all they were worth in a vain bid to reach the trailing reins which were now dragging on the ground between the hoofs of the team.

'I can't reach 'em, Hoyt. What'll I do?' Parsons yelled out to his partner.

The driver did not hear him. Hoyt's lifeless left arm fell limply down before the rest of his body followed it into the belly of the box.

'Hoyt?' Parsons shrieked at his dead friend. 'What am I gonna do?'

More screaming came from inside the coach. A woman was crying out through a mixture of panic and agony. More bullets found their target as the guard stared down at the team of horses which were totally out of control. They were now nothing more than a terrified and powerful team of animals hellbent on escaping the fear which pursued them. Trying to free themselves from the shackles which held them in check.

Without the expert guidance of the old driver the stagecoach was now rocking precariously as its half dozen horses ploughed off the trail and through every obstacle in their path. A wall of trees were now directly ahead of the harnessed team and their helpless freight.

Parsons swallowed hard. He knew he had to try and stop this vehicle at any cost if any of them were to survive. Hoyt had known there was only one way to do that without the reins and that was to get down between the alarmed horses. To leap from the box and pray that you landed on the moving traces without falling beneath the hoofs of the frightened team. Parsons swung a leg over the lip of the driver's box and balanced for what felt like a lifetime. He had to jump: there was no other course of action. He kept glancing up through the choking dust at the trees. Trees which were getting ever closer as the horses carved a route through the tall grass toward them.

The stagecoach guard gave his dead friend another look. He heard the frantic screams of the passengers inside the coach beneath him and then exhaled. He returned his eyes to what lay below him.

His eyes were glued to the wooden pole as it swayed on the chains of the team's harness. It was not a large target for a man to jump on to as it convulsed between the galloping horses.

The stagecoach thundered on toward the trees.

Fearlessly, Snub Parsons jumped.

THREE

The seasoned guns of the outlaws still spewed their lethal venom at the fleeing stagecoach even though it was obviously out of control and headed toward disaster. Holstering their smoking weapons the gunmen dug their boots into their stirrups, leaned back and dragged their mounts to a halt. Their cold emotionless eyes watched as the stage-coach careered off the dusty trail and hurtled through the tall grass toward a wall of trees a hundred or so yards away.

The breathless Grant Largo steadied his horse as his four gang members gathered around him. 'In a few moments we'll have the strongbox, boys.' he wheezed before pulling a twisted cigar from his coat pocket and ramming it between his blackened teeth.

Tracy struck a match along his saddlehorn and cupped its flame in his gloved hands. He said nothing as Largo leaned across the distance between their mounts and sucked the flame into the end of the long brown cigar.

'Kinda funny.' Vance Largo sniggered. 'Seeing all that horseflesh trying to kill themselves and all them folks.' None of the others responded.

The terrain was uneven and rugged away from the well used valley trail. The stage was rebounding as one after another its springs broke beneath it. Luggage bags flew off the roof in all directions as its team of feverish horses forged on in blind terror.

A terror which could never be outrun but was matched by the screams of the passengers trapped within it. The coach had never been designed for this kind of punishment and was breaking apart the further away from the trail it went.

To the men who looked on, there could be only one conclusion to what they were witnessing: the total destruction of the stagecoach when it eventually crashed into the distant trees.

Yet what none of the five outlaws could see was the guard fighting to get to the lead horse of the team and the stray reins, which he knew were his only chance of stopping the vehicle before it collided with the immovable wall of trees.

In all the years he had been a shotgun guard, Snub Parsons had never even considered what he might be forced to attempt to do if anything ever happened to his driver. Now that very occurrence was happening and he was totally committed. Committed to trying to stop six crazed creatures who were thundering out of control. It was like attempting to walk a high wire in a tornado but Parsons kept on heading between the horses as his boots balanced perilously on the moving wooden pole and his hands gripped anything within reach.

The speed of the coach was totally beyond anything Parsons had ever experienced before. He knew he ought to be afraid but there was no time. No time to be anything but determined. He felt his boots being bucked off the wooden traces and he clung on to anything available just to stop himself from disappearing down into the void where he knew the horses' hoofs would crush him to a pulp.

The guard could see the loose reins of the two leading horses flapping around ahead of him. He had to reach them. Parsons held on to the closest of the horses' padded collars and then swung his legs forward. He propelled himself forward between the middle pair of horses. This time he managed to grab hold of the chains which hung across the backs of the galloping animals. His boots slipped off the slippery pole. His legs fell into the gap to the right side of the thundering horse and it took every ounce of his strength to clamber back up until he felt his feet locate the traces once again.

Exhausted, Parsons glanced ahead.

The trees were now closer. Too close for his liking.

He had less than a minute to achieve his goal, to stop the team from killing themselves and probably everyone else on what was left of the stagecoach.

The guard clawed his way forward by using the chains to either side of him. His hands were torn to shreds as the crude metal tore at his flesh but he kept moving ahead until he was close to the tails of the lead horses.

He leapt like a mountain cat at the very same moment that the coach behind him was thrown up into the air and then came crashing down on to its side. But the horses did not slow or stop. The team continued to drag the now upturned vehicle on its side through the unforgiving grassland.

Then the bloodied Parsons heard the pitiful passengers' screams. It was like being spurred. Although he had no time to think of anything except the problem in hand he glared at the loose reins with gritted teeth. He ran along the pole, leaned over and scooped them up into his bleeding hands. Without even thinking he wrapped them around his left arm and leapt off the gyrating trace pole.

Parsons found the lead horse's collar. He swung his entire body on to the horse's wide back. The trees were coming at them faster now. Without even knowing what he was doing he looped the reins around the horse's neck and pulled backward with a power he had not even imagined that he possessed.

The lead horse was being strangled.

Strangled into submission.

'Stop, you son of a bitch,' Parsons blazed. 'Stop.'

The mighty lead horse obeyed. It dug its forelegs into the ground as it battled with the guard who was throttling it. When it stopped, the five other horses were forced to reluctantly do exactly the same.

The team came to a halt within a few feet of the first of the trees. Snub Parsons sat for a couple of seconds on the back of the sweat-sodden animal and then fell off on to the grass.

He lay there staring at the stagecoach on its side and listening to the now muted cries coming from within the wrecked vehicle. The limp body of Hoyt was hanging from the edge of the driver's box. The old timer's legs had been skewered by the shattered brake pole.

'This ain't good,' Parsons muttered to himself, as he tried to force himself back to his feet.

He was on his knees when the sound of gunfire filled his ears again. The guard lowered his head and began to curse.

Bullets cut through the dust which still hung on

the clean crisp air close to the high pines like a swarm of crazed hornets. Red hot tapers of death trying to finish the job the Largo gang had started less than ten minutes earlier tore into the bark of the trees directly behind the spot where the guard knelt. A cloud of hot sawdust fell over the horses and the man.

Another salvo followed less than a heartbeat later.

Parsons felt their heat above and around him. Only the high swaying grass which had been spared the brutal onslaught of the careering horses and stagecoach protected the bruised and battered guard now.

'Damn it all,' Parsons snarled as he tried to shake the dizziness from his blood-soaked head. 'Don't them varmints know when they've won?'

More shots erupted. To his horror two of the horses closest to him gave out pitiful whinnies as the outlaws' bullets tore into their sweat-sodden flesh. Parson's eyes narrowed as he saw the lead horse buckle. Blood issued from the random holes in its neck and poured out in warm arches all over the guard. The wounded creature would have fallen on top of the stunned Parsons if not for the harness which glued it to the rest of the team.

The still groggy Parsons reached down to his holster. His bloody fingers vainly searched for the six-shooter which had disappeared long ago during his heroic leap and climb between the team of horses.

'Damn it all.' The guard again cursed as he heard the unmistakable sound of horses' hoofs approaching. 'Of all the times to lose ya hogleg.'

Urgently Parsons rubbed his face. He had to wake up. He had to regain his thoughts, he silently told himself. When they spotted him he'd be as dead as old Hoyt.

He swung on his knees as another volley of bullets ripped into the trees which now faced him. Splinters showered over the man as he crawled through the grass to where his weary eyes made out a gap between the trees.

More shots rang out behind him.

It was as though every bone in his body was hurting at the same time but Parsons kept crawling. He did not look back. He dared not look back. If he saw them, they would surely see him and take aim. They had guns and he had nothing but bruises. He ignored the agony and continued to crawl. He fell on his belly but still kept crawling.

The sound of the riders' laughter filled his ears as the horses drew closer to the upturned stage.

He had to escape.

Every instinct in him told him he had to escape. He had to survive to fight another day. Another day when he had guns to help even up the odds.

He was no coward but he was not a fool either.

After crawling for twenty yards through the long grass like a sidewinder, Parsons reached a deep ravine filled with every known type of flesh-tearing weed an unlucky man could encounter. Without hesitation he rolled down into it. He knew that the pain from the thorns which ripped through his clothing and flesh was nothing compared to what the death-dealing outlaws' guns would do to him should they locate him.

'Gotta live to fight another day, Snub,' Parsons muttered to himself over and over again. 'Gotta live and teach them bastards a lesson.'

Then Parsons heard another sound from his unholy sanctum. A sound which drowned out the laughter of the riders. It was their guns exploding into action once again. The trapped six-horse team were now the outlaws' targets. Their lethal guns blazed into deafening fury as Largo and his gang finished off the rest of the coach team for no better reason than they could. They had the power to do so and they did.

Snub Parsons felt sick.

He closed his eyes and covered his ears with his bloody hands in a vain bid to block out the next even more nauseating sound which found his hiding place.

The rugged guard was only too aware that two of their three passengers that morning had been women. Respectable women somewhere in their thirties, he had guessed. Now it was their turn to shriek out for a mercy which would not be granted.

No matter how much Parsons pressed the palms of his hands against his ears he could not prevent their heartbreaking screams from filling his head.

Even though it was not he who was hurting them, Parsons felt personally guilty and responsible. He was a stagecoach guard devoid of all his weaponry and forced to listen instead of protecting them. He was hurt and yet the pain which racked his every movement seemed little more than a pitiful excuse to him.

Even though he had risked his very life just to stop the coach from crashing into the trees, he still blamed himself for what had followed.

He had failed.

Then the outlaws' laughter grew even louder. It was the laughter of retched creatures who had satisfied their carnal appetites like mindless animals. He had heard it before during the bitter conflict when men suddenly became little better than the lowest of creatures and violated anything remotely feminine their basic urges wanted to. Old women who should have earned respect were used to satisfy uncontrollable lust. Even small children who should have been regarded as sacred were not safe from those kind of creatures, he recalled.

Parsons could taste the bile in his mouth.

The trophies of war. The strong over the weak. No words could ever convey the true horror some men brought upon those they had bettered.

It had sickened Parsons then and it still did.

Memories of the sights which always accompanied the sounds filled his thoughts. He had spent years trying to forget and now it was all flooding back.

Parsons tried to get up from his sanctuary but the brambled vines held him down.

The Devil was making him listen.

Satan wanted him to remember.

Wanted him to recall how evil could, and often did defeat the good. How the beautiful innocence of purity could be crushed beneath the heels of the wicked.

Snub Parsons gritted his teeth and forced himself back on to his feet. The thorns had ripped his flesh. Blood ran freely down his length from head to toe but he did not feel it.

Then he heard the victorious cheers and the sound of hoofs as the outlaws spurred away from their conquest.

Parsons paused. He knew he was too late to do anything.

Tears filled his eyes and travelled down his weathered features washing tracks of blood in their flow. It was not the physical pain which was now hurting him, but the memories.

Memories of a time all sane men tried to forget.

Racked by uncontrollable guilt, he clawed his way out of the ravine.

FOUR

On the steep trail leading down into the valley rider and horse had become one living entity. A score of years had been swept away from both of them. The sure-footed horse thundered ever downward with precise skill and confidence. Even after the sound of distant gunfire had ended, the horseman urged his mount to continue. The damp soil of the steep tree-covered mountainside was treacherous. It slipped away from under the hoofs of the tall stallion but it did not slow its furious pace down to where the land was flat. As though his boots were glued into his stirrups Trask shadowed every movement of his confident charge. Defying their years the pair had twisted and turned as one and negotiated the perilous pathway down to the belly of the valley in break-neck time.

Upon reaching the lush grassland which led to

the dusty trail cutting through its middle, the horseman had urged his mount to find even greater courage and speed. The old stallion had not been found wanting of either.

Carrying Trask high on its shoulders, Smoke had ploughed a furrow through the fertile terrain until it eventually reached the almost bleached yellow road. A road where the keen-eyed Trask had spotted the disruption to its dusty surface. The tell tale marks of the thundering stagecoach and its pursuers were still fresh. Still remained.

Yet for all of the speed both horse and master had displayed, Trask knew that they were already too late. The gunshots had ended long before they had managed to reach the well used road.

Whatever had happened was now history. A mere memory like the lingering reminders of the gunshots which had drawn them down into the valley in the first place. The unknown gunmen were probably well on their way to seek out their next innocent victims. Their next prey.

It was hard for Trask to accept that they were too late but every seasoned sinew in his body knew it to be the truth. The bitter truth. They had been too far up the side of that mountain to ever reach those that needed their help in time, but men like Trask had to try.

The famed gunfighter continued to hang on to his saddlehorn with one hand and swing his free arm in urgency so that his old horse would keep up its blistering pace. As always old Smoke did not let its master down.

Dust curled up off the stallion's hoofs and lingered in the air behind them as they raced along the road towards the still rising sun. The heat greeted them but neither man nor beast gave it any heed. They simply raced on.

Trask had begun to think that the road had no end when he saw the very thing he had been searching for. The first sign of what had happened.

A dozen yards ahead the brutal reality of their futile quest came into view. The mighty stallion was hauled to a stop at the spot where the stagecoach had veered off the road. Steadying his loyal mount, Trask stared at the scarred ground. He became angry. Angry with himself for not being able to reach this place in time, to have altered the outcome. Trask rose off his saddle. He balanced in his stirrups as his wise eyes surveyed the clues of what had occurred an hour or so earlier.

Dust floated around both horse and rider as the famed gunfighter sighed heavily and gripped his reins. He glanced into the tall grass and could just make out what was left of the stagecoach a hundred yards from the road. He sensed that death lay out there amid the high swaying grass.

How much death was still to be determined. Trask steadied the nervous animal beneath him as its flared nostrils detected the scent of blood hanging on the morning air.

Trask looked down with studious eyes. The clues of what had occurred were carved out in the road and the grass. He could see the grooves left by the stagecoach's metal wheel rims where they had torn into the softer ground. The high grass had been flattened by the team of six horses and the hefty burden they had dragged across the otherwise pristine ground.

It was all there for educated eyes to see. Eyes which had seen too much of this before. But it was not the brutal scars left in the wake of the fleeing stagecoach which drew Trask's observance the most, it was hoof marks a few feet ahead of his stallion.

The seasoned rider could see that at least five horsemen had stopped their mounts and watched from the edge of the road where the ground was far moister. The hoof marks buried deep into the mud. These were not the hoof prints of the fleeing out of control stagecoach team. They definitely belonged to the outlaws who had attacked the coach.

Trask knew that the outlaws had steadied their horses here and watched the horror unfold before them. A horror of their making. The horseman sighed. Less seasoned men might have been concerned that some of their number could still be prowling around for fresh prey, but not Trask. It had taken him the best part of an hour to descend the mountain trail and reach this point. Far too long for even the most evil of souls to lie in wait. Trask felt sure that whoever had caused this mayhem had probably been after the strongbox on the coach and once they had gotten their hands on that they would have headed on their way. He allowed his horse to walk beyond the hoof marks and then saw the crushed grass a dozen yards further up the road where the riders had returned from gathering up their loot. Grass and muddy clumps littered the sandy coloured road.

Trask squinted along the road.

'That's where them varmints went OK, Smoke.' Trask muttered to his weary horse before turning it full circle to face the flattened grassland again.

Trask pulled his reins with his right hand. The stallion turned and stepped down into the ploughed up grass. Patting the neck of the stallion, the gunfighter urged the tall animal on toward the scent of death. After a few paces Trask could also smell it. The morning sun was higher now and its heat was filling the heart of the valley. There was death ahead, Trask silently told himself. What kind of death and how much was yet to be figured out.

The stallion began to shy. The sickening aroma was getting stronger.

'Keep going, Smoke. Ain't nothing to be feared

of.' Trask whispered as his eyes darted all about him looking for potential danger. He knew he was an easy target. All tall men on even taller horses were damn easy marks to the fearful or just plain evil souls who confused guns with heroics. 'Nothing 'cept some hurt critter that might think we're the same evil bastards that caused this, boy.'

As always Trask had been right to be wary.

The snorting stallion had barely covered twenty yards when Trask heard the distinctive sound of shotgun hammers being locked into position. The horseman reined in, quickly lowered his upper half over his canteen and then slid off the horse into the cover of the high grass. Trask felt that whoever it was out there with the shotgun it was more than likely the stagecoach guard or driver.

Even if he were correct, it made the weapon no less lethal.

Trask held on to his reins tightly and listened again. Sweat trailed down his weathered features as the gunfighter considered the situation he had willingly ridden into. Yet Trask did not reach up for his holstered guns hanging over the neck of his horse.

This was not one of the outlaws who had forced the stagecoach off the road into this wild grassy ocean, Trask kept silently telling himself. This was one of the injured people who had been on the ill-fated vehicle. They had to be injured. Nobody

43

could have survived the wreckage he had caught a glimpse of and not endured injury.

Trask removed his Stetson, wiped the sweat from his brow along his sleeve and considered his options. As though trying to convince himself, he reasoned again that if it were one of the outlaws out there with the scattergun he would have already been cut in half by its twin barrelled fury.

It had to be one of the stage's crew.

He returned his hat to his head when more nerve rattling sounds filled the air. These were different to those of the scattergun being primed for action. Trask listened intently.

They came from further along the ripped up terrain. From close to the upturned coach. Muffled and indistinct they raised the hair on his nape. If pain had a sound Trask had just heard it. The gunfighter eased himself back up until he was level with the shoulder of his chestnut mount. He leaned forward, screwed up his eyes and peered out under the neck of the tall animal.

The overturned coach was twenty or so yards from where he and his horse stood. He had thought that he had seen it just before he had heard the sound of the gun hammers and dropped to the ground.

His eyes vainly searched the area but the grass was too high for him to see whoever it was who had cocked the hammers of the shotgun.

Then the haunting noise resumed. Suddenly Trask realized what the sounds were. It was the whimpering of women. At least two of them. They were hurt and that roused the gunfighter into wanting to help. He straightened up and looked over the mane of his chestnut.

Questions burned into Trask's mind.

Where was the gunman?

Was his judgement impaired by his injuries? Would he fire blindly at Trask if the gunfighter moved out unprotected into open ground?

Again his eyes searched for the man who had cocked the shotgun. A man who just might let loose with both barrels.

Trask heard the pitiful cries again. He had to do something before death ended those whimpers permanently. He had already arrived too late to stop this from happening. Trask could not allow his own fear to prevent him from doing something.

'Easy, Smoke. I gotta go and face up to that scattergun-toting *hombre*.' Trask allowed the horse to slowly walk on as he leaned against his saddle and kept looking out from over the neck of the tall stallion. Each step brought him closer to the stage-coach wreckage; closer to the whimpering noises; closer to the man who held on to the scattergun with bleeding hands; closer to death itself.

Although he did not know it, Trask had been

right on all counts concerning the man who had cocked the hefty weapon in readiness.

Snub Parsons was scared and he was also injured. After returning back to the scene of the Largo gang's brutal outrage, he had dug his hefty scattergun from out of the driver's box and upon hearing the approach of the stallion Parsons had decided it was healthier to be safe rather than sorry.

The guard swallowed hard but there was no spittle in his dry mouth to ease his throat's soreness. He mustered every ounce of his nerve and yelled out.

'Stop right there, mister.' Parsons instructed from behind the wreckage of the coach. 'I'll surely kill ya if ya don't.'

Trask did as ordered.

The veteran gunfighter paused and looked across the distance between himself and the man standing beside the coach with the twin barrelled weapon clutched in his shaking hands. Trask frowned when he saw all the blood covering the guard.

'Don't go firing that cannon. Ain't no call to be feared of me, pard,' Trask called back. 'I only come here to try and help.'

'Who are ya?' Parsons yelled back nervously. 'I don't recollect ever setting sights on you before. Who are ya? Tell me the truth. I ain't in no mood to be joshed with.'

'I can see that, pard,' Trask retorted. 'Ya looks like ya hurt real bad there.'

'I am.' Parsons agreed. 'Now tell me ya name.'

'They call me Trask.'

There was a lingering pause before the shotgun guard spoke again. It was clear as spring water to the gunfighter that the man who had him in his sights had heard of the name. What he had heard was another matter though.

'Trask? The famous *hombre* called Trask?'

'That's right, pard.'

'How'd I know that ya really Trask?' The uneasy guard questioned. 'Anyone can say they're some-body like Trask. Don't mean that's who ya really are.'

With raised arms high Trask stepped away from the stallion. 'Look at me. I ain't got my guns strapped on, pard. I don't mean ya no harm and I just come spurring 'coz I heard the shooting. Sounds like ya got hurt womenfolk over yonder. Let me see if'n I can help them.'

Parsons pondered the voice. It sounded older than he had considered the famous gunfighter would be. He squinted. The sun was behind Trask. The stranger looked nothing like the guard had imagined anyone as famed as Trask would look.

'Ya damn old, mister. How can I believe ya really Trask? He's a legend and you're just a withered old man.'

Trask gave a slight laugh.

'Even legends get old, pard.'

'You say ya ain't wearing ya guns?' Parsons edged away from the coach with his hefty weapon clutched firmly in his bloody hands as its twin barrels were levelled at Trask. 'The grass is too high. I can't see if ya telling me the truth or just bluffing. Head on this way so I can see ya better. Remember, I'll cut ya in two if ya try anything.'

Trask did as he was instructed and walked toward the guard as the stallion followed. Within five paces both men were facing one another. Parsons looked at the thin figure with his arms raised high. His eyes then darted to the horse and the gunbelt hanging over its neck.

'That ain't a darn smart place for ya to have ya guns, mister,' the guard noted.

'I only strap them on when I need to use them,' Trask told his interrogator.

With the scattergun still aimed at the gunfighter, the guard ventured closer and stared at the face of the man who was roughly the same height as himself. 'Are ya the real Trask, mister?'

'Yep.' Trask nodded. 'Take a close look at the guns and the belt. Got my mark on that belt, pard.'

Snub Parsons supported the wooden stock of his weapon on his hip and stepped up to the stallion. His eyes focused upon the grip of the closest Colt jutting from the holster. Then he looked at the hand-tooled gunbelt. He stepped even closer and his eyes widened. He gasped in awe.

'Holy cow,' he gulped before returning his attention to the gunfighter. 'The mark of Trask.'

FIVE

Trask waded through the broken debris left in the wake of the thundering horses and wrecked stage-coach closer to the front of the upturned conveyance. Saplings were split and grass flattened as though a twister had cut through the normally pristine terrain. Yet it was none of this which caught the keen eyes of the gunfighting legend. It was the blood which greeted his boots every few steps. So much blood it confounded the seasoned man who sought out the women who were still crying.

At first Trask did not see them hidden in the swaying grass close to the wreckage. The tall thin man paused as the guard reached his shoulder. The sight chilled his ancient soul.

Trask had witnessed many atrocities in his long life but none of them had prepared him for what he found in the grass. Even wounded by bullets which had splintered through the wooden walls of the coach and cut into their flesh, both women had proven irresistible to the Largo gang's carnal desires. Trask said nothing as he studied the women's torn clothing which barely remained upon their bodies. Their under garments had been ripped from them and were scattered all around the place where they had been mercilessly used. Every scrap of their dignity lay strewn around them. The collective stains left by their rancid attackers dried on their flesh and festered inside their bodies. Blood stained their naked legs but this was not the blood resulting from wounds created by either bullets or the crash. This blood was more evidence of what the nauseating stage-coach robbers had done to them. Both women whimpered like whipped animals unable to under-stand the unspeakable savagery they had endured. Their minds were as broken as their bones.

'Damn it all.' Trask sighed quietly. 'What kinda vermin are we dealing with here, Snub?'

There were no answers.

The guard placed a reassuring hand on Trask's wide shoulder and also sighed heavily. The gun-fighter glanced at the injured Parsons and gave a slow nod. Neither man spoke further as they viewed the pitiful women. There were no words capable of describing the unholy apparition they both looked upon. No words which could even come close.

Filled with a mixture of pity and uncontrollable

anger, Trask inhaled deep and long and turned away. Then he cast his eyes on the place where the sickening smell was coming from. The acrid scent increased with every passing heartbeat as the blazing sun grew higher and more intense above the scene. The six horse team had been riddled with bullets as they had stood in their traces. Flesh had been torn from their hides by the ferocity of the outlaw's lead. Flies had already found the carcasses.

Then Trask saw the limp body of the driver impaled on the broken brake pole. He just hung in mid air like a side of beef on a butcher's hook.

'There's the body of a man inside the coach,' Parsons told the silent Trask before adding: 'Them critters blew his head clean off.'

'I figure this gang was after ya strongbox, pard.' The gunfighter kicked at the ground. 'They get it?'

'Yep.' Parsons rubbed his neck with his brutal-ized hands in dismay and confused outrage.

Trask glanced back at the slaughtered horses.

'Why'd they kill the horses, Trask?' the guard asked as though the legend would have the answers his own brain could not provide. 'Ain't no call to kill a whole team of horses. Not like that anyways.'

'Why'd they do any of this,' Trask ventured.

'I just don't figure none of this,' Parsons said.

'Tell me. What happened exactly, pard?' Trask asked.

'We was on our regular trip from Gold Falls to Mohawk Flats and had only bin in the valley for about half an hour when five riders come out from the trees a few miles back.' Parsons tried to explain. 'They opened up and just wouldn't quit until old Hoyt got plugged and dropped the reins into the traces. The stagecoach went out of control and left the road. I jumped down from the box on to the poles and tried to reach the reins. But I only just managed to get them and stop the team when them varmints started shooting again.'

'Ya a brave man, pard,' Trask noted before turning his attention back to the two women. 'Mighty brave.'

'Brave?' Parsons repeated the word. 'I high-tailed it for cover like a scared rabbit when the shooting started again, Trask. Is that brave? I'm just a yella belly.'

Trask bit his lower lip. 'No yella belly ever jumped between a galloping team of horses and tried to get hold of their reins, Snub, boy. Ya lost ya guns and had a choice to make. I'd have done the same.'

'Ya would?' Parsons gasped.

'Yep.' Trask gave a firm nod.

Parsons pointed at the women. 'But look what them bastards done to those little ladies, Trask. I could have stopped them if I'd stayed here and not. . . .'

'They'd have killed ya the same as they done to these horses, pard,' Trask told his companion firmly. 'They'd not have given ya a chance before they'd slaughtered you.'

The guard gulped. 'So I ain't a coward?'

'Not in my book.' Trask began to walk to where the women lay sobbing. Again he paused and looked at the far younger man who matched his every step. 'We gotta get them to the nearest town. Is there any place around here where we can borrow a flatbed buckboard?'

Parsons looked back toward the road. 'Yeah, there sure is, Trask. Old man Riley got himself a horse ranch about a mile up into the hills. He'll surely have one.'

Trask patted the shoulder of his blood-stained comrade. 'Take Smoke and ride like the wind to that ranch and tell them what's happened and borrow a buckboard. We have to get these women-folk to a sorebones real fast by the looks of them.'

'What about ya guns?' Snub Parsons pointed at the gunbelt hanging across the neck of the stallion. 'Ya want me to get them for you?'

'I don't need them right now.' Trask answered. 'Go get that buckboard.'

The guard nodded with renewed confidence. 'Ya can count on me, Trask. I'll not let you or them ladies down.'

'I know that, pard,' Trask sighed. 'I know that.'

SIX

The day still had an awfully long way to go before the sun would finally decide to set, before the mindless killing would eventually end. Flanked on both sides by countless trees, Mohawk Flats was a small quiet town set almost exactly halfway along the length of Mohawk Valley. Like so many of its contemporaries it was virtually self contained. It even had its own small brewery set close to an ice cold river where just enough beer was made each day to satisfy the town's thirst.

Just shy of three hundred citizens lived and worked within its boundaries and they catered for all the small ranches which lined the fertile land set between the high mountain and the rolling tree-covered hills. Anything the people of Mohawk Flats could not create with their own hands was brought in by stage or covered wagon.

In all the time since the first pioneers had set

down roots, it had never experienced a whole lot of trouble. People here lived their lives without envy or vengeance. Without even knowing it, they had found an Eden. They all bided their time and knew that time itself would heal all of their problems. A white washed church sat at the end of the main street with its cast iron bell hanging in its cradle high in its impressive spire. Like so many churches it mainly drew the women and children to be preached upon whilst the majority of the town's menfolk went about the more physical and practical sides of their lives. Husbands, fathers and brothers all knew that their women could handle more than their fair share of the spiritual side of things for all of them.

All in all Mohawk Flats was a peaceful place.

That was all about to end.

The hot afternoon sun was directly over the town as the people of the small settlement went about their daily formalities. None of them seemed to notice the five horsemen who appeared out of the heat haze along the dusty road and steered their mounts toward the first of its wooden buildings.

Mohawk Flats seldom had call to even think about the troubles of the outside world and had no idea of what the five riders had in store for them. With little contact with strangers how could they even comprehend what dangers these five outlaws posed to each and every one of their number?

These were gentle, naive souls.

Like animals who have no natural predators they knew nothing of the evils which lay outside Mohawk Valley. All knowledge of such things had long been forgotten. They had no fear of anyone or anything. For fear is something which is learned by brutal experience.

These people had only experienced tranquillity.

Grant Largo and his four followers had their pockets filled with the money which they had relieved the discarded strongbox of a few miles back down the road. Yet as the five foxes entered the hen house known as Mohawk Flats they began to sense that just like the women they had vituperated earlier, these people would offer no resistance to anything they dished out.

All five riders noted that none of the town's menfolk carried weapons or wore gunbelts as was usual with most other towns in the West.

Perhaps they thought that they did not need weaponry. Until the arrival of the five horsemen, they had been correct.

As the blazing sun shimmered the air before them, the Largo gang began to realize they had discovered the perfect place to unleash their own brand of evil. If these townsfolk thought they were safe, the riders would willingly prove them wrong.

The main street meandered in a fashion akin to

many others they had ridden down. It was as though buildings were erected wherever trees permitted, for it took a long time to fell a stubborn tree and it had always proven far easier just to add a slight bend in a street rather than waste time and effort with axes.

The welcoming scent of honeysuckle was everywhere along the thoroughfare but none of the outlaws noticed. They had other thoughts on their crude minds; thoughts of how they could take this town for all it had. And by the looks of it, Mohawk Flats had plenty to take. There was unexploited wealth here to be had by those who wanted it badly enough. There were also plenty of women of various ages who had yet to be contaminated by the poisonous appetites of the strangers within their midst.

The elder of the Largo brothers was first to spot a saloon halfway along the crooked road. A smile came to his rugged features as he aimed a trigger finger at it. All five steered their mounts toward the drinking hole.

As the horsemen reined back each of them had noted that there appeared to be no sheriff's office anywhere to be seen. Largo looped his right leg over the cantle of his saddle and lowered his bulky frame down to the dusty street. He gripped his reins tightly in his hands and studied every living creature within sight before securing his leathers to the saloon's hitching rail.

Jumping down from his weary mount, Tracy knotted his reins and stepped up on to the boardwalk outside the saloon and rested his knuckles on his gun grips.

'Did ya notice, Grant?' Tracy asked his leader as the larger man stooped beneath the pole and joined him on the creaking boards.

'Yep, Pete,' Largo replied drily. 'No law to be seen.'

Tracy beamed to reveal his broken teeth. 'I'm liking this place more and more. We can sure have us a wild old time here and no mistake. Ain't nobody gonna blow our candles out before we sets light to this town.'

'Damn right.' Grant Largo nodded.

O'Mara swung his leg over the neck of his horse and slid down to the ground. Dust encircled his boots upon impact. 'Might be law down one of these side streets, Grant.'

'There might be but I surely doubt it,' Largo agreed as he watched his brother dismount and toss his reins loosely over the rail. 'Knot 'em, Vance.'

The younger Largo paused and stared wildly into his brother's eyes as though ready to draw on him. 'What ya say there, brother Grant?'

Grant Largo looked at the reins and then back at his troublesome sibling. 'Ya heard me, boy. I told ya to knot 'em. Knot 'em tight.'

Defiantly Vance tilted his head. 'And why would I wanna do that for, brother?'

'Why? Two damn good reasons.' Grant Largo growled. 'The first reason is that horses are like you. They're dumb and wander off. Ya don't wanna come running out of here and find ya horse is halfway to Waco, do ya? The second reason is that if ya don't I'll kick that smile off ya face. Savvy, Vance boy?'

The younger of the Largo's looked like a coffee pot close to boiling over. He snatched at his leathers and then knotted them as tightly as he could to the pole. 'That good enough for ya?'

Grant Largo nodded slow and long. 'Yep.'

Keets remained astride his horse. Flies seemed to linger wherever the deadly gunman tarried. He kept looking up and down the street as though memorizing its every feature for future reference.

'Ain't ya thirsty, Keets?' Tracy asked.

'Something mighty wrong with this town, Pete,' Keets muttered with a wave of his free hand. 'Can't seem to figure what but something ain't right.'

'Nobody got no six-shooters on their hips, Keets.' Grant Largo said.

Keets started to smile. 'Yeah, that's it. They're all walking around like they was preachers or the like.'

'Ya coming in now, Keets?' Tracy grinned.

The gunman dismounted and tied his reins next to all of the others along the hitching rail. He stepped up and shook his head as though still unable to grasp the fact that none of the residents of Mohawk Flats was armed. 'Damned strange place this, boys. They must have religion or something. I done never seen so many menfolk without guns before. Ain't natural.'

The Largo gang entered the saloon. The swing doors rocked on their hinges as the five brutal killers walked slowly across the fresh sawdust toward the bar. The saloon was empty apart from the barkeep and a few old men seated close to the door.

There was an ominous murmuring within the confines of the saloon as the five dust-caked outlaws strolled deliberately toward the balding wide-eyed bartender. The customers finished their suds and then departed as quickly as their legs could carry them. The swing doors again rocked.

The barman had been enthusiastically polishing beer glasses until he looked up as he saw them. Then the glass fell from his hands and smashed into a hundred fragments at his feet. He gulped and tried to rest his shaking hands on the bar counter but they refused to stay put.

'H-howdy, gents,' he managed to say.

Grant Largo reached the counter first and raised his right boot and rested it upon the brass rail close to a spittoon. His own gloved hands remained close to his gun grips as his eyes darted at what was on offer behind the bar.

'Ya got any redeye?' Largo asked in a threatening tone.

The bartender took a step backward toward two wooden kegs. He managed to point to them. 'W-we got beer, sir. Lots of good beer.'

The five outlaws looked at one another. There was a sense of unspoken disappointment which lingered.

'No whiskey?' Tracy asked.

The bartender slowly shook his head and tried to smile but his face was frozen with fear. 'Only beer. Brewed in town. Fresher suds ya can't find any place.'

'What kinda town is this?' O'Mara spat at the spittoon.

'Not many folks around here care for strong liquor,' the bartender informed. 'Besides, it'd have to be brought in here by wagon and there just ain't the call.'

Vance Largo pulled out his tobacco pouch and loosened its drawstring with his teeth as his eyes burned into the small man across the bar. 'I say we kill this varmint.'

A look of total bewilderment filled the features of the bartender. 'I-I ain't to blame, gents. Hardly no one even likes whiskey in Mohawk Flats.'

Keets had not spoken since reaching the counter. He continued to remain silent as he strolled around to the end of the bar and raised the wooden flap. The face of the bartender began to twitch as the fragrant outlaw started to walk toward him.

'Please don't hurt me,' the bartender quietly begged knowing that the only way to escape was to leap over the counter and his leaping days were long behind him. He backed off but Keets continued to walk at him with a strange twisted smile carved into his dirty features.

The bartender felt the end of the wooden counter stop him as he reached its end. He was trapped and he knew it. The front of his pants started to darken as fear weakened his bladder.

O'Mara pointed at the damp patch on the front of the barkeep's pants and laughed. 'Careful, Keets. He might just drown ya if he gets any more feared.'

'Please don't hurt me,' the bartender again begged as his fingers interlocked as though in prayer. 'Please.'

Keets did not stop walking until his body was pressed up against the far smaller man. The stench from his shinning clothes wafted up into the trapped bartender's flared nostrils. Keets raised a finger and touched the end of the man's nose, glaring down into his tear-filled eyes. 'Ya said there's hardly no call for whiskey, *amigo*. Hardly sounds like there is some call but maybe not a whole lot. Which is it?'

'S-some folks drink it.' The little man admitted.

'Where'd they drink it at?' Keets' breath was even worse than the stench of his unwashed clothing.

'Here.' The bartender confessed as his shaking finger pointed at a box under the belly of the counter. A dusty box two feet square. 'They drinks it in here.'

Keets eased back and reached under the counter. He dragged the box out and then placed it on top of the counter. The sound of bottles filled the interior of the saloon. Each of the outlaws looked at one another as wry smiles etched their faces.

'Is that what it sounds like, little man?' Keets whispered out of the corner of his mouth at the cornered barkeep. 'Is this a box of hard liquor?'

'Y-yes, sir,' the sweating barman admitted. 'They ain't belonging to the saloon though. I can't sell them. They belong to a few of the town's menfolk who leave them here.'

Eagerly Keets dragged the lid off the box and stared into it. There were ten full bottles of whiskey sitting beside a half-empty one. Keets tilted his head and stared at the trapped man. 'So ya lied to us?'

'N-not really.'

'Kill him.' Vance Largo ran his tongue along the gummed edge of his cigarette paper and pushed the twisted smoke between his lips. 'I say ya kill him, Keets.'

Keets watched as his cohorts helped themselves to the bottles and then pulled one from the box for himself. 'I surely ought to kill ya, *amigo.*'

'Please don't,' the bartender pleaded. 'I got me five kids and I'm a widower. I only work here.'

Keets pulled the cork with his teeth and spat it across the room. At exactly the same moment his right hand moved with such speed that none of the others even saw him draw and cock his six-shooter. They did, however, see and hear the weapon as it burst into action and sent a bullet between the smaller man's eyes. A funnel of gore exploded out of the back of the bartender's head when the bullet exited his skull.

Keets had holstered his weapon even before the body of the bartender had hit the floor. He took a swig and laughed out loud. 'Now them five kids is orphans, boys.'

Vance stood on the brass rail and leaned over the counter, grinning wildly at the dead man. 'That'll teach ya to lie to the Largo gang.'

'He won't do it again, Vance,' O'Mara noted.

With the resounding echo of the shot still ringing in his ears, Grant Largo filled a beer glass with whiskey and stared at it longingly. 'Reckon that should have well and truly woken up the whole town and no mistake.'

'Ya figure on trouble, Grant?' O'Mara asked as he lowered his own bottle from his cracked lips.

'Yep. A heap of trouble and I'm the bastard that's gonna start and finish it all, Snipe.'

With hands resting on his holstered gun grips, Pete Tracy turned and faced the bright sunshine beyond the swing doors of the saloon. 'I figure we'll be mighty rich by the time we finish with Mohawk Flats, boys.'

'Did ya see all them women out there?' Vance gushed as he struck a match across the top of the counter and cupped its flame. 'We're gonna be mighty tired as well by the time we finish with all of them.'

'Reckon they'll fight back, Grant?' Tracy wondered.

The elder Largo shook his head. 'Nope.'

The men all laughed. It was a sickening laugh.

SEVEN

The unfamiliar scent of gunsmoke filled the twist-ing street as it drifted out on the afternoon air over the swing doors of the saloon. Its acrid fragrance had drawn people from all corners of Mohawk Flats to the main street. A mixture of curiosity and fear burned into their souls. There was a disbelief in them. Apart from fireworks on the fourth of July, none of the townsfolk ever heard anything remotely resembling a six-shooter being dis-charged within earshot. Only hunters used their rifles up in the forests which flanked them on both sides and that was only ever for game.

The chilling noise of the solitary gunshot had long faded but still hung in the stunned souls of everyone who had heard it. Now they inhaled the odour left in its wake. There was confusion in Mohawk Flats: what was happening? Who had fired that gun and why? A lot of questions and not one answer.

Slowly they gathered together in small groups along the boardwalks beneath the verandas of the various structures which made up main street. An unknown terror filled each and every heart which pounded.

Some of those who had been close to the saloon when Keets had brutally killed the bartender knew where the shot had originated yet none of them had the courage to investigate further. Whatever evil was inside the saloon would remain unhindered.

As the outlaws had guessed, there was no law or lawmen in the remote town but there was a crude form of governing council. Tom Jacobs, the mayor, had been in office for nearly twenty years because no one else had ever wanted the job. He had always managed to strike the right balance for all of the town's people and businesses but now they wanted him to guide them into something he had no knowledge of.

Jacobs had been almost dragged from his small office at the back of the hotel he owned and bustled along the winding boardwalks until he was standing outside the hardware store directly across the wide street from the saloon. Scores of voices asked him questions whilst an even greater number were advising him what he ought to be doing.

So many voices. All aimed at one man. It had

become a muffled crescendo where all the voices blended together until nothing was heard except deafening noise.

The 49-year-old mayor found himself unable to do anything except stand open mouthed, watching the front of the only saloon in Mohawk Flats. He did not have a clue what he should be doing because nothing like this had ever happened in the town before.

In fact Jacobs could never even recall a time when a gun had been fired in town. He was astounded and utterly incapable of action.

'Ain't ya gonna do nothing?' A voice from the crowd shouted at Jacobs.

'We want answers,' another bellowed.

'Somebody must go and see.'

'Do something, Tom. Do something. Anything.'

'Ya yella, Tom. Always have bin. Damn yella.'

The mayor went to answer when even more hostile jibes came at him from all directions. Jacobs was thunderstruck. He had never seen these people so riled before. It frightened him. If the sound of one shot could do this to these people what would they be like should even more shots ring out?

Jacobs raised his arms and began to try and restore order.

'Easy, folks,' he implored. 'Now who heard the shot?'

69

A dozen arms went high.

'Where'd it come from?'

'The saloon.' Most of them said together drowning out those who had other suggestions of the shot's location.

The mayor saw the comforting face of Doc Bunston and stepped toward the tall figure. 'You actually heard the shot, Doc?'

'Sure did, Tom.' Bunston nodded as he sucked on his pipe and searched his pockets for tobacco to fill its bowl. 'Scared the pants off me.'

Jacobs leaned closer to the far taller man. 'And it came from the saloon?'

'Yep.' The doctor gripped the stem of his pipe with what teeth remained in his mouth. 'Ain't no doubt about that, Tom.'

'Are ya certain it was a gun?' Jacobs pressed. 'It weren't no firecracker or. . . .'

'It was a gun, Tom,' the doctor said confidently. 'It was a hand gun. I'm sure of that. I heard enough of them back in Tombstone when I was there. Ya never forgets the sound of hammer on bullet, boy.'

Jacobs rubbed his jaw and bit his lip. 'Damn.'

The troubled crowd seemed to be growing as more and more people were lured to the place they felt certain the shot had emanated from. They gathered around the mayor until he was forced to sit down on a chair outside the hardware store. His glazed eyes fixed on the faces he no longer seemed to recognize. In all his days in Mohawk Flats he had never seen them like this; they were frightened.

Frightened of the unknown.

Their imaginations were running riot creating scenarios each more terrifying than the last. The mayor was worried. Not by the unseen gunmen inside the saloon but by what the normally quiet townspeople might do. He had heard tales of crowds running amok when fear filled their minds.

'Ya gonna do something, Tom?' Doc Bunston asked the man with his face buried deep in his hands.

Jacobs looked up at the doctor. 'Did ya see the strangers who own them horses over yonder, Doc? Did ya happen to get a look at them?'

Bunston glanced over his shoulder at the saloon and the five lathered up horses tied to the hitching pole outside its swing doors. 'Nope, Tom. I never seen them arrive. The first time I even noticed them nags was when that shot rang out.'

Jacobs stared at the unfamiliar mounts and rose back to his feet. He brushed aside the women and children until he was hovering on the edge of the boardwalk. 'Anyone know whose horses they are? We have to try and figure this out. Maybe someone just got himself a tad excited over there and sent a bullet into the ceiling. Just 'coz we heard a shot it don't mean anyone got hurt.'

Bunston patted the shoulder of his troubled friend. 'I sure hope ya right, Tom.'

'Why don't ya go over and take a look, Tom?' A churlish female voice asked the mayor from behind the wide shoulders of some of the towns menfolk. 'Scared ya might be wrong and them strangers might shoot you as well?'

Jacobs shook his head. He tried to ignore the mocking words but they burned into him like branding irons. He went to answer when a boy no more than eight pushed his way through the crowd and tugged at his pants leg. Jacobs looked down.

'What ya want, Bobby? Can't ya see we got a problem here, son?'

Bobby Carter was a child who lived mainly on the streets rather than in the home he shared with his parents and seven siblings. His clothes bore the signs of a child who liked to play hard. Yet unlike so many other of the towns children Bobby had a maturity only blessed upon those who live by their wits.

'I seen the riders of them nags, Mayor Jacobs,' the boy said.

Jacobs crouched down until he was able to look the child straight in the eyes. 'Ya did? Who was riding them horses, Bobby boy?'

'Strangers. Real mean looking strangers,' the boy started. 'I heard one of them call another

Keets. Another was called Pete. They had more guns in their belts than I ever dreamed anyone would have. Why'd they need so many guns?'

The question was one Jacobs asked himself. Why would strangers have so many guns? No respectable cowboy needed an arsenal. All he would require was a rope and a good horse. These strangers sounded as though they might be wanted men. A chill traced down the mayor's spine.

The mayor gripped the shoulders of the boy. 'What else did ya hear them saying, Bobby?'

'They said something about noticing that none of the men in town was wearing guns. They seemed real happy about that. They all laughed.' The child took in air and then carried on. 'How come they'd be so happy just 'coz none of the men in town wears guns, Mayor Jacobs?'

'They were all wearing guns?' Jacobs asked the child. 'Are ya sure they were all well armed, Bobby?'

'Yep. I never seen so many before,' the boy confirmed. 'They had fancy gunbelts filled with bullets all shinny too.'

Jacobs patted the boy's face gently and then rose back to his full height. His face was grim as he looked into the faces of those who surrounded him. They had all heard the innocent words spoken by the boy.

'Who fired that shot?' The booming voice of the

preacher called out, as he strode down the board-walk toward the crowd of troubled people.

Everyone turned and looked at the pompous sight of Philo Tewksbury as he headed toward them. The stick thin figure clad in traditional black attire, more suited to an undertaker, waved a hand in which he held a Bible.

'Tell me who has dared to fire a weapon in Mohawk Flats, Mr Mayor.' Tewksbury stopped a yard from the weary Jacobs and continued to rant as only certain types of men can. 'This is an abom-ination. Which one of you is guilty of this outrage?'

Jacobs looked the preacher up and down. 'Don't ya ever get tired of thinking ya better than the rest of us, Philo? Any critter who can read can read out of the Good Book. It sure don't make ya better than us.'

'How dare you.' Tewksbury stepped forward and pushed the Bible into the mayor's face. 'The Lord will punish you for casting shadows on one of his servants, Jacobs.'

Jacobs pushed the man away and returned his gaze upon the saloon and the five restless horses still tethered outside its swing doors. 'Pray for me, Philo.'

'What?' the preacher regaled.

Bunston stepped between the two men and pointed his pipe at the saloon and bent down to whisper in Tewksbury's ear. 'The shot came from inside the saloon, Philo.'

'The Devil dwells in there,' the preacher raged, waving his fist at the saloon. 'All who enter that place shall burn in the bowels of hell.'

Unable to conceal his contempt, Tom Jacobs glanced at the preacher. 'Must be damn tough being righteous all the time, Philo.'

The preacher went to speak again when his head was jolted back by the left hand of the mayor. Jabobs' eyes narrowed as he glared at Tewksbury.

'I told ya to pray for me, Philo,' Jacobs repeated.

The preacher was shocked into silence even after the hand was removed from his face and he watched the mayor turn and start walking straight at the saloon.

A united gasp went through the crowd.

'What's he doing?' Tewksbury asked.

No one answered.

Watching the unarmed mayor bravely walk toward the saloon, Doc Bunston gave a long sigh. 'Reckon I'd better go to my office and get my bag. I got me a feeling that I'm gonna need it real soon.'

EIGHT

Ten miles from the tension which now gripped the people of Mohawk Flats the legendary Trask was soaked in his own sweat as he laboured amidst the wreckage of what had once been one of the Overland Stagecoach company's finest vehicles. Since shotgun guard Snub Parsons had ridden off to find a flatbed buckboard to ferry the dead and injured to town, Trask had been busy. Ignoring the nagging pain in his guts he had managed to drag the headless body of the coach's male passenger out of the upturned vehicle and lay it down next to the remains of old Hoyt. In all his days of riding the untamed West, Trask had never witnessed as much mindless carnage as this and his work was still not done.

The dead were one thing but it was the living who now posed his biggest problem.

To the crazed and tortured minds of the two

women all men now came from the same sickening breed as those who had brutally defiled them. Noticing that one of the women had also been shot, Trask had tried, unsuccessfully, to approach them twice before. Chewing on his failure, he had then turned his attention to the dead men in a vain attempt to try and think of how he could help the petrified women.

Both times their fear of being harmed even further had filled the countryside with their hysterical screams. Trask could face anyone with a gun but he had always shied away from shrieking women.

He rubbed his gloved hands down his shirt front and again stared at them. Trask knew the two women had been brutally assaulted and required urgent help. Their flesh had been ruptured by the savage outlaws as the five men had spent themselves like stud stock, taking it in turns to satisfy their depraved urges. Even having at least one bullet in her had not saved one of the women from the attack.

The veteran gunfighter had located a large waterbag in the long grass where it had been thrown when the coach had crashed on to its side. Trask had carried it on his shoulder the fifty yards back to the women and then again tried to consider a way he might gain their trust.

'They call me Trask.' He said as he ventured

again to where they still lay bleeding. One of the women shook where she lay as though having a fit. Trask knew that time was against them.

One careful step after another brought Trask to within ten feet of them. Then their startled eyes darted at him.

He stopped. His only consolation was that this time neither of them screamed. Maybe they saw that he was not wearing any guns or perhaps it might have been his voice. His voice which matched his appearance.

'I thought ya might need some water to drink and wash yourselves down with, ladies,' Trask said calmly. 'The guard took my horse to find a wagon so we can take you to town and find a sorebones. Reckon there might be some ranchers with Snub when he gets back though. It seemed to me that you might want to cover up before them men see you.'

Their reaction was as before: terror. This time silent.

'I'll place this down here,' Trask said lowering the bag of water down on to the grass. 'I could try and find ya bags so that you got some clothes to replace them ripped ones.'

Trask backed away and then stopped once more.

One of the women suddenly clambered up to her feet. What was left of her clothing fell away leaving only the remnants of a bodice covering her upper half. Cuts and bruises blanketed her flesh. From the dark mound of hair roughly eight inches below her navel evidence of knife marks could be seen. Dried blood stained the length of her legs to her ankles, yet she seemed totally oblivious of any of her injuries. It was as though the softly spoken words of Trask had brought her out of the trance she had been trapped within. She stepped away from her travelling companion.

She looked straight at Trask with innocent eyes.

'Who are ya? Ya ain't one of them.' She said as though a curtain had been lifted from her. 'Ya different.'

Embarrassed, Trask averted his eyes and then removed his hat respectfully. 'No, ma'am. I ain't one of the dogs that hurt ya both. I'm called Trask. I just come to try and help but I was too far away to get here in time to stop what them men done to you. I'm mighty sorry about that.'

The woman seemed totally unaware to the fact that she was completely naked from the waist down. She walked through the grass toward him. 'You're old.'

Still keeping his eyes trained on the ground Trask nodded as she reached him. 'Yes I am, ma'am. Darn old.'

'You have a kind face though.' Her fingers touched his weathered features. 'Sometimes age befits a man. Gives him a look of wisdom.'

79

'Getting old sure makes ya bones ache though, ma'am.' Trask smiled.

'My names Martha Stewart. I'm the school mistress at Mohawk Flats,' she informed. 'At least I will be when I manage to get there.'

Trask looked into her eyes. He cleared his throat. 'Ya want me to find some clothes for you, ma'am?'

'Oh. Oh dear.' Suddenly she looked down at herself. She blushed as though she were far younger than her actual years. Her tiny hands vainly tried to conceal her modesty before she dropped down and crouched in an attempt to protect herself from prying eyes. 'I'm so sorry. I don't know what has happened.'

He placed a hand briefly on her hair. 'Don't fret none. I'll find them bags, Martha.'

'I'm so sorry. What must you think?' She frantically apologized. 'I remember now. I bumped my head. My friend has been shot. I remember now. Oh dear. Those awful men. They. . . .'

'I know,' he whispered.

'I'm so ashamed.' She started to weep.

'Ya don't have to be, little lady.' Trask vowed, 'They'll pay for what they done to you and everyone else.'

Her tears stopped rolling down her cheeks. She believed his every word.

Trask turned just as he heard the distant sound

80

of approaching horses and a buckboard. He began to run to where he thought he had seen a canvas bag. 'I'll go find ya bags. Reckon ya got time to dress before Snub gets here.'

Martha Stewart prayed he was right.

It was the longest walk that Tom Jacobs had ever taken. The heat of the blazing sun burned down on the reluctant mayor as he forced himself across the wide empty street toward the saloon. It was as though a score of invisible chains were slowing his every step but he forced himself on. This had to be settled, he silently told himself over and over. This had to be resolved one way or the other. More than a hundred people watched in silence as Jacobs finally reached the secured horses and briefly paused beside them.

His heart was shaking inside his frame. He was terrified of what he might encounter beyond the swing doors of the saloon.

He reached a hand down into the trough and rubbed the warm liquid over his neck and then reluctantly stepped up on to the boardwalk. Sweat trailed down his features from sodden hair as he inhaled deeply and placed a hand on top of one of the swing doors and looked into the saloon.

The five owners of the tethered horses were still inside its dark centre. Grant Largo remained at the bar counter sipping at his large glass of whiskey, whilst the other four men were seated at a card table. Each of the gang members had a half consumed bottle of hard liquor before them.

Jacobs narrowed his eyes and looked for the bartender. There was no sign of the frail balding man. He had no idea that the crumpled corpse of the bartender still lay where it had fallen after Keets had shot him.

One by one the outlaws spotted the anxious mayor standing behind the suspended doors. Well fuelled smiles greeted him.

It was Grant Largo who spoke first. 'Looks like we got ourselves a visitor, boys.'

Largo's younger brother stood and gripped his holstered guns ready to draw and fire them both if given the nod by his elder.

'Easy, Vance,' Pete Tracy said over the rim of his whiskey glass. 'He ain't no threat to us.'

'Rest ya bones, boy,' O'Mara added. 'It's just a nosy local critter with either more guts than he oughta have or he's just plumb loco.'

Keets laughed.

Confused, Vance glanced at his sibling. Grant Largo gestured with his left hand for his brother to sit back down. The fiery youngster did so and, plucking up his bottle, started sucking on its neck again.

The older Largo gripped the handle of his glass and walked across the sawdust littered floor until he was a few feet from the man standing just outside the entrance to the saloon. Grant Largo stretched his neck and looked over the swing doors at the man who had braved instant death just to feed his curiosity and then nodded. 'Neat critter, ain't ya?'

Jacobs cleared his throat. 'I'm the mayor. Reckon I have to be a little neater than most folks.'

Largo smiled and placed a hand on the door not gripped by the white knuckled Jacobs. He pulled it toward him.

'Come on in, Mr Mayor,' Largo said.

The mayor swallowed hard and did as he was told. His feet shuffled like those of a man twice his age. They did not want to enter the lion's den; they wanted to turn on their heels and run for the safety of the watching crowd.

'Thanks,' Jacobs said automatically as Largo released his grip on the door and it swung back.

'So you're the mayor?' Largo muttered, as he circled the man standing a couple of yards from the table where the four others watched.

'Yep. Duly elected.' Jacobs nodded, trying to ignore the sweat which now sought and found his eyes. The salt burned and he began to squint. 'There was a shot in here and the folks yonder was a tad troubled. They was wondering a few things.'

'What things was they wondering about?' Tracy asked with a wide grin on his face.

The feet of the mayor shuffled. They still wanted to high tail it out of the saloon.

'Things like who fired the shot and why,' Jacobs managed to say without one single word faltering as it left his lips and found their ears. 'That sort of thing.'

'I killed the barkeep, Mr Mayor,' Keets announced waiting for a reaction which failed to happen. 'Any objections?'

It took every scrap of his resolve not to start running but Jacobs did not move from the spot. He glanced at the long bar counter. 'Is his body over there?'

'Yep.' Keets nodded.

A wry chuckle went around the table.

'Why'd ya kill him?' Jacobs found the courage to ask.

'I felt like it.' Keets spat.

'Duly elected, huh?' Grant Largo muttered as he continued to circle the troubled mayor with his glass held close to his mouth.

Jacobs nodded firmly. 'Yep. Unopposed.'

'Nobody else wanted the job, huh?' Keets piped up from his chair. 'Must be a real bad 'un.'

'Unopposed?' Grant Largo repeated the word.

Jacobs looked at the hardened face as it passed in front of him for the umpteenth time. 'Indeed.'

'We gonna kill him, brother Grant?' Vance slurred.

Largo looked at his brother. The look stopped

his sibling from uttering another string of words.

Jacobs felt the hair on the nape of his neck rise. He was now more scared than he had been when he had watched the awesome figure of Grant Largo approach him. He went to speak but his throat refused to work.

'Scared?' Largo asked.

Jacobs nodded.

'They sure elected a mighty dumb mayor.' Tracy laughed.

Largo stopped right before the mayor. His eyes burned into Jacobs as they inspected the unarmed man carefully. 'Ya might be wondering why I walked around ya, Mr Mayor. Well the thing is I seen many a dude hide guns in all sorts of places to try and git the drop on me. I was just checking that ya was not packing.'

'I have no guns,' Jacobs said before wondering if his words might be wasted on men who already knew the truth.

'Are ya brave or just loco?' Largo asked.

'Neither,' Jacobs replied.

'Curious?' Grant Largo raised a bushy eyebrow.

The mayor nodded. 'I must admit that I was curious to see who had ridden into our town.'

'Do ya recognize us?' Largo asked.

'I've never seen any of you boys before.' Jacobs sighed. 'How could I recognize folks I've never seen before?'

Keets pushed his bottle away from him on the wet table and tilted his head and gave the mayor a long hard stare. 'There ain't no law in Mohawk Flats, is there?'

'We've never required any lawmen.'

Keets turned to face the three other seated outlaws with a broad smile on his filthy face. 'No law. No Wanted posters.'

The three others all laughed loudly.

Jacobs blinked a few times. 'Are you wanted?'

Grant Largo leaned into the mayor until their faces were so close that a cigarette paper could not have separated them.

'Dead or alive, *amigo.*'

NINE

The sickening sound of the feasting flies gorging upon the dead horses' carcasses filled the otherwise quiet place where the stagecoach had come to rest. The smell and sound of death was now overpowering but the gunfighter did not seem to notice either outrage. All he could think about was catching up with those who had done this. Catch up and then punish them.

Trask was tired, though. Dog tired. It had been many years since he had found himself in a situation remotely like the one he was now embroiled in. Age now dictated his every move and yet he had found himself doing things far better suited to someone at least a decade younger.

The only sign of Trask's weariness was in his weathered features – his face was ashen. He had helped Snub Parsons hoist the dead bodies on to the back of the flatbed buckboard without uttering a single word of complaint. Then he had helped the guard assist the pair of injured women on to the borrowed conveyance before turning his back on the bloody reminders of what he had been unable to stop. For men like Trask it was as though he himself had been party to the outrage itself; guilt of not being in the right place when needed haunted the gunfighter.

Thirty minutes earlier Parsons had arrived back at the wrecked stagecoach with the buckboard and two cowboys from the nearby ranch but there was nothing any of them could do except give comfort to the women and respect to the two dead men.

The guard could see that Trask was troubled. Troubled by something the younger man could not understand. For the one thing which Trask had not given even the slightest of clues about was the fact that the nagging discomfort deep inside his innards had returned.

This time it had returned with the ferocity of a jagged knife. It had no mercy in it. No respect for the legend who was known throughout the West as Trask.

But the gunfighter would never mention it. He would simply continue on as he had always done. Forging ahead to right the wrongs evil bestowed upon the weak.

Stagecoach guard Snub Parsons had not known this stranger long but felt as though he knew the character almost as well as he knew himself. If ever he wished to emulate any other living man it was Trask.

Moments earlier one of the cowboys had ridden off toward Mohawk Flats to alert the doctor that he had a couple of wounded customers headed his way. The other cowboy had realized that there was nothing he could do to help and returned back to the ranch set up in the hills.

Without even knowing why, the younger man followed Trask to where the coach had come to a brutal stop only an hour or so earlier.

'What's eatin' ya, Trask?' Parsons innocently asked.

Trask turned. Their eyes met. The seasoned gunfighter did not reply but kicked at the ground for the umpteenth time. There were no words which could convey the frustration felt by the veteran drifter. Nothing which could give a clue as to how much pain he was in.

The guard closed the distance between them. Trask was forced to look at his companion long and hard.

'Ya look ill, Trask.' Parsons noted.

Again Trask did not respond.

'Ya coming into town with me?' the younger man pressed. 'I reckon the varmints that done this might be there already and I sure ain't hankering to tangle with them again.'

89

Trask thought about what he had seen here. Then he narrowed both eyes and gave a nod. 'Yep. I'm riding old Smoke right into town with ya, Snub.'

A relieved Parsons walked shoulder to shoulder back to the buckboard and then began to wonder if all the tales he had heard over the years about this famed man were actually true. He looked to his left at the face of the thoughtful man.

'So ya reckon on trying to find out who done this to these people, Trask?' the innocent guard asked as he reached the tailgate of the vehicle.

'I ain't gonna try and find 'em, Snub,' Trask corrected. 'I am gonna find them.'

'Then what?'

'Then I'll face them down.' Trask replied drily. 'One by one or all together. It don't worry me which it'll be.'

'A showdown?' Parsons gasped.

Trask gave a slow nod. 'If that's what they calls it. Yep. A showdown.'

'But what if they're faster than you?' Parsons sounded uneasy. 'There must be about six of them. That's a heck of a lot of firepower to try and better. Can ya outgun that many?'

Reaching the back of the buckboard, Trask pulled its gate up and secured it with iron pins. He then walked to where his mount was tethered and yanked its reins free. With every stride the younger man was with him. Finally as the gunfighter was about to step into his stirrup Parsons grabbed hold of Trask's elbow and stopped him in his tracks.

'Hold on there, Trask. Ya might be a mighty famous critter and I'm just a nickle and dime shotgun guard but when I asks a question I'd like me some courtesy. Answer me.'

Trask looked at the hand and then into the face of the confused man. 'Pardon me all to hell, Snub. I thought we was through gabbing. These gals need to be taken to a sorebones damn fast.'

Parsons stared hard at Trask. He knew that the man beside him was ducking the question. 'Are ya figuring on taking on all six of them bastards alone?'

Trask pulled his arm free and then mounted the tall stallion and gathered in his reins. 'There's five of them, Snub. I counted the tracks.'

'Huh?'

'Five. Not six. Just five.' Trask turned the chestnut horse and glared out toward the dust left by the cowboy who had ridden for Mohawk Flats a few minutes earlier.

'Five outlaws against an old man,' Parsons whispered bluntly so that the females would not hear his concern. 'That's suicide in my book and ya knows it.'

A smile came to Trask's face. He patted the gunbelt and its hard-crafted holstered weapons.

91

'Ya wrong, Snub. Five outlaws against the guns of Trask.'

Snub Parsons' eyebrows rose as he tried to work out what the experienced gunman meant. 'Talk sense. Guns are just guns.'

'Not these.' Trask ignored his pain and smiled at the concerned face. 'They're special. They'll not let me down. They never have.'

'What? Ya trying to tell me that these guns are magic or something?' Parsons could not tell if Trask was joking or serious. 'That's loco talk.'

Trask put all his weight on to his left stirrup and gripped his saddle horn with his right hand.

'Git up on the plank, boy. Ya gotta drive this wagon all the way to town.' Trask leaned over and grabbed hold of the younger man's arm and hoisted him off the ground until the guard's boots found the driver's seat of the flatbed. Parsons scrambled on to the well sprung plank and then gathered up the long leathers of the two horse team.

'Ya gonna take them all on, ain't ya?' Parsons asked. 'Ya gonna try and outgun them five deadly critters.'

'Yep.' Trask swung the loose ends of his reins and then brought them down at the ground. A cracking noise filled the air and the buckboards team took off with their driver holding on for dear life.

Trask watched the buckboard kicking up dust and then ran a hand down the neck of the stallion beneath him. He straightened up and rubbed his aching stomach. He still hurt. Hurt bad. But there was no time to fret over things he had no power over. All he could think about was finding the outlaws who had killed those men and defiled those ladies. When he found them he would teach them a lesson and make them pay.

He sighed and lifted the gunbelt off the horse's neck and wrapped it around his middle. Trask buckled it and then adjusted the holsters until they were against his thighs. He tied the long laces firmly around his legs and gave out a long sigh.

How many times had the veteran gunfighter followed this same ritual?

How many more times were left for him to repeat this simple action – to ready himself and front up to potential death?

Few men had ever faced so many adversaries in their lives and survived to tell the tale. Trask glanced at the road ahead of them and knew that this just might be the final time. Were the guns truly special as he had grown to believe them to be? Would they find their targets as they had always managed to do or would this be the time when Trask would discover he had always been wrong?

Would it take his own death to prove to Trask that it had always been him who had been fast on the draw and not the guns themselves? Only his own death would destroy his irrational belief in the matched Colts, the guns which he had long thought had protected him for most of his grown life.

The seasoned gunfighter knew that there was no more pain once you were dead. He rubbed his flat guts again.

Trask loosened the reins he had wrapped around the saddle horn and inhaled long and deep. The pain seemed to ease a little as he stood in his stirrups.

'Come on, Smoke. We got us a score to settle.' He urged the horse to begin the long ride toward the distant settlement. As always the magnificent stallion obeyed its master blindly.

Dust curled up into the blue sky off the hoofs of the striding animal as it gained pace. Trask gritted his teeth and balanced in his stirrups.

'One more time,' Trask shouted.

TEN

Johnny Dukes had been a wrangler for all of his
adult life and there were few who could ride quite
as well as the 25-year-old. The youngster had
driven his quarter horse along the dry trail from
the stagecoach crash to the outskirts of town with
the haunting memory of the injured women and
two dead men burned into his mind. He knew that
one of the women was hurt far worse than the
other. She had not only been savagely assaulted
but shot in the side. The poor creature had been
barely conscious when Dukes had thrown his lean
frame atop his mount and spurred for Mohawk
Flats.

There was urgency in the horseman's wrists and
spurs as he thundered along the last quarter of a
mile toward the first of the towns buildings. To his
surprise there did not seem to be any people
within sight. The wrangler steadied and slowed his

95

powerful mount when he saw the faded wooden shingle hanging on a rusted chain from the porch overhang. Every local man, woman and child in the valley knew that it belonged to the cantankerous Doc Bunston.

Dukes hauled rein and almost flew from his saddle before landing on the boardwalk to face the approaching medical practitioner as the older man reached his home and front parlour office.

'Are ya loco, Johnny?' Bunston railed back as the panting cowboy came to an abrupt halt before him. 'I could have had me a heart attack being shocked like. . . .'

'Doc,' Dukes gasped as he tried to suck in wind. 'Thank the Lord I found ya.'

'Out of the way, Johnny,' Bunston frantically gestured, before passing the dust-caked figure. 'I have to get my bag and head on back to main street. There's gonna be some shooting if my old bones ain't telling me lies.'

Dukes swung on his heels as the doctor passed him. 'There's already bin shooting back on the road to Gold Falls, Doc. Two dead and one woman darn close to heading that way herself.'

Bunston stopped and looked at the panting cowboy. 'Slow down, Johnny. What ya trying to tell me, boy?'

Dukes waved a finger back at the dust left hanging in the air off the hoofs of his mount. 'The stagecoach was attacked. The driver is dead and so is a male passenger. Couldn't tell who he was on account that his head was blown clean off. There was two womenfolk on the coach and the robbers done hurt them real bad. One is looking awful bad.'

The doctor turned the knob of his front door and entered his parlour which was also his office. The cowboy trailed him like an obedient hound to the desk where a well worn black leather bag rested on a pile of paperwork.

'I ain't joshing ya none, Doc,' Dukes insisted.

'Shot you said?' Bunston looked hard at the cowboy. 'One of these women has been shot in the side?'

'Yep.' Dukes nodded earnestly. 'I never seen so much blood, Doc. She'll need ya cutting her open to get that lump of lead out, I reckon.'

The doctor ran a slim hand across his neck. He was thinking hard as all men of his profession tend to do when knowing that a mistake of judgement could cost a life.

'So ya want me to go out there?'

'No, Doc.' Dukes waved his hands. 'They're bringing her and the other lady in on a buckboard they borrowed from my boss.'

Bunston went to the table where he always operated. It was covered with months of dust and newspapers. He removed it all with one sweeping movement of his left shirt sleeve. Dukes said nothing as the doctor kicked the rubbish into a corner.

'Head on across the road and see if Ma Smith is there, Johnny,' Bunston said masterfully. 'Tell her to head on over here with some boiling water. Tell her I'll need her to help me when I operate on that wounded lady. Understand?'

'Yep.' Dukes nodded and raced out into the sunshine toward the doctor's old nursing assistant's home.

Doc Bunston returned to his desk, opened his bag and stared at the fine set of instruments he had owned since first gaining his degree decades earlier. 'I gotta make sure these things are sterile,' he told himself.

Without warning the echoing sound of a gunshot being fired somewhere back down in the centre of the remote town filled his ears.

The doctor's long thin legs marched to the open door. Bunston rested the palm of his left hand on the wooden frame as his eyes searched vainly up toward main street.

As with the earlier shot there were no following blasts from other deadly weapons. Again it had been just one single shot.

The cowboy ran back from Ma Smith's small neat house. As he ran, he too was looking down toward the place where the noise of the shot had come from.

Dukes slowed and then stopped next to Bunston. 'Ya hear that, Doc?'

'Yep. I heard it, Johnny. I sure hope I'm wrong but I got me a feeling that we might have to elect us a new mayor.' The doctor sighed before returning into the shade of his parlour. 'C'mon, boy. I need ya help.'

The cowboy, again, obeyed.

ELEVEN

The grey putrid smoke trailed from the barrel of Keets' raised gun and twisted in the rays of sunlight which cut across the otherwise dim interior of the fly filled saloon. The stinking shootist gave a twisted, drunken laugh, twirled the weapon on his index finger until it found its holster once again. Keets then dropped back down on to his chair and nodded to himself before glancing up at the figure of Largo.

'OK, Grant?' Keets asked.

'Yep.' Largo ran a thumbnail across his whiskered jaw. 'Ya plugged him real fine, Keets. Real fine.'

It was a horrified Tom Jacobs who staggered and then buckled in agony. The hole in his left thigh went clean through his leg. As the man collapsed on to his knees, blood started to flow from the smoking holes left in the wake of the accurately placed bullet. Tears filled his screwed up eyes as the mayor gaped at the grinning Keets sat next to his three cohorts. Keets lifted his whiskey bottle back to his lips and started to gulp what remained of its fiery contents with satisfied glee.

'What ya wanna go do that for, ya bastard?' The mayor spat at the sawdust which surrounded him. Sawdust that was starting to turn red, as blood flowed from between his fingers and down his pants leg to the floor. 'I never done nothing.'

Grant Largo towered over the kneeling figure. 'Keets was just trying, in his own way, to make ya realize that when we asks questions, it ain't healthy not to answer real pronto. Savvy, Mr Mayor?'

Jacobs looked up at Largo. 'What questions? Ya never asked me none.'

Largo grabbed hold of the man's hair and hauled it toward him. The neck of Tom Jacobs almost was snapped by the powerful exertion. 'Ya weren't listening, fella. I asked ya how much money ya got in that bank of yours. Remember?'

Jacobs knew that it was pointless arguing. Not with men fuelled to the gills with hard liquor. These were men who were deadly when sober and far worse when they had whiskey in their innards.

'I'm s-sorry. Ya right. What I bin trying to tell ya is that the bank ain't really a bank at all,' Jacobs retorted before dragging his black tie from his shirt neck.

The seated men at the card table all began to chuckle as they watched the blood covered fingers of the injured man attempt to stem the flow of the blood from his wound.

Unlike the others, Grant Largo saw no humour in the statement. None at all. He tugged at the hair of the mayor even harder. Jacobs was almost lifted off his knees. He dropped the gore covered tie on to the floor.

'Now ya talking in riddles, Mr Mayor,' Largo growled. 'A bank that ain't a bank? How drunk do ya figure we are?'

'Listen to me,' Jacobs pleaded. 'What I meant to say was that it ain't like a regular bank building. We ain't never had the call to have no bars or even a safe. It's just an ordinary house. Clem Barker runs it for the rest of us.'

Grant Largo released his grip and pushed the mayor forward brutally. Jacobs fell on to his face as the large outlaw moved to his gang with the widest smile on his face any of them had ever seen.

'Did ya hear that, boys?' he joked.

'I heard.' O'Mara grinned.

'Sounds like we really found ourselves the end of the rainbow, Grant.' Tracy slapped his leg. 'I never heard the like before. Sounds like we better not puff too hard or it'll fall right down.'

Vance Largo rested his chin on his knuckles on the table. 'I don't git it. What the hell are ya all laughing about?'

Ignoring his brother, Grant Largo swung around and looked down on the pathetic figure before him. Blood was everywhere. It circled Jacobs as the man vainly tried to get back up on his feet.

'Sad sight,' Largo noted.

'Pitiable,' Keets added.

Tracy looked at his empty bottle and frowned. 'Ya gonna let that sad varmint keep bleeding all over the floor like that, Grant?'

Vance Largo dragged one of his guns from its holster and tried to pull its hammer back. 'I'll kill him for ya, brother Grant.'

'No,' Grant Largo argued.

The younger of the brothers stared through blurred eyes at his sibling. 'Hell. Ain't ya gonna let me kill nobody today, Grant?'

'Holster that hogleg, Vance,' Grant Largo ordered before he looked down at the man covered in his own gore. The outlaw then shook his head before staring back at the blinding sunlight of the street. He could hear the women out there. Women he knew could be theirs for the taking. 'We might need this critter alive, little brother.'

Snipe O'Mara stood and walked around the table to where his leader stood. 'Ya figuring on us staying in this town a tad longer than we'd planned, ain't ya?'

The older Largo ran a gloved hand across the face of O'Mara. 'Sometimes, Snipe, I reckon ya almost as smart as me.'

Vance Largo pushed his gun back into its holster and rocked on his chair in a vain bid to keep his eyes open. 'Can I kill me someone later on?'

Pete Tracy patted the back of the man sat next to him. 'Don't go frettin', boy. They'll be plenty of killing to do before we leave this town.'

Largo looked at the mayor. 'Tend his leg, Snipe. I wanna keep this critter alive. I reckon he'll open up a whole lotta doors for us.'

'Ya figure there's any whorehouses in Mohawk Flats, Grant?' O'Mara leaned over and hauled the bloody mayor off the floor and helped Jacobs to a chair. He removed his bandanna from his neck and then knelt and tied it tightly above the bullet-holes.

Grant Largo grinned and moved to the swing doors and looked out over them. He could see the women out there; lots of them of all ages and sizes. 'We don't need no whorehouses, Snipe. I figure the spineless men in this snivelling town will be more than willing to give us their wives and daughters just as long as we don't kill them.'

O'Mara got back to his feet and rubbed the blood off his hands down his sides. 'When we gonna start?'

Grant Largo looked at their prisoner. 'As soon as that poor sorrowful critter gets his wind back, Snipe.'

The others stood and began checking their hardware.

Jacobs looked up from his chair and stared through his bedraggled hair at the five outlaws who had him and the rest of Mohawk Flats at their mercy.

His heart sank.

No heaven-sent bolt of lightning could have stunned the people of Mohawk Flats more. The nauseating sound of the second shot coming from within the saloon sent a renewed panic spreading like a wildfire through every man, woman and child in the town's main thoroughfare. The crowd backed off for the relative safety of lanes and alleys as soon as they had heard the resounding gunfire inside the saloon.

Fear now outweighed curiosity. None of them wanted to risk being hit by a stray lump of lead if it happened to miss its chosen target and carve its way through the weathered wooden façade of the saloon.

A collective gasp had swept through each of the onlookers and none of them would have placed a bet that their brave mayor was not already lying dead.

The thin man who still clutched his well thumbed Bible remained on the edge of the boardwalk directly across the street from the saloon. Philo Tewksbury had turned preaching into an art form over the years. A way of imposing his will over the less flamboyant majority of the town's people. But now the preacher felt as though all of his words would mean nothing unless he somehow acted.

Jacobs had acted but now it seemed as though it had cost the mayor his life. Tewksbury however could not envisage the same fate happening to him for he had God on his side.

Over years of bestowing countless God-fearing sermons to his flock the preacher had come to believe the pietistic words that flowed so easily from his lips as if they had come straight from his Maker. Relishing in the delusion that he had direct contact with God made Tewksbury more than a mere man; Philo Tewksbury actually believed that he was blessed and protected by the God he had long preached about in the remote settlement.

The preacher stared at the saloon.

Everything he had ever despised was within that weathered structure. His mind raced as he listened to the words which filled his thoughts. Words which told him to be unafraid. Words which told him that he could not be harmed by the Devil's evil disciples.

106

With only his Bible as protection Tewksbury was about to step down and walk toward the tails of the five tethered horses when a familiar voice carved into his mind.

'Who bin doing all the shooting, Preacher?' The massive Ralph Ford had walked the long distance from his livery stables at the edge of town with a hefty hammer resting on his muscular left shoulder. Men like Ford wrestled with ornery horseflesh and bent steel into shape for a living. Little else frightened their breed.

The sharp question made Tewksbury turn his head and look at the approaching man who defiantly marched down the very middle of the street.

'Get over here, Ralph,' the preacher demanded.

Ford stopped and stared at the thin figure and then at the crowd of townsfolk who were still hiding in the gaps between the buildings. 'What's going on here?' Ford boomed as only huge men could.

Tewksbury frantically waved his hand and arm at the blacksmith. 'You'll git shot, ya darn fool. Git over here before they spot ya.'

There was no hint of alarm in Ford as he reluctantly obeyed the instructions and wandered slowly toward the porch uprights the preacher was hiding his stick thin frame behind. The preacher grabbed hold of the large man and vainly attempted to pull him to safety.

'Ease up, little man. Ya ain't gone loco, have ya?' Ford asked as he stepped up beside the Bible-toting man. 'Who'll shoot me? Who?'

A shaking hand pointed at the saloon. 'The Devil's in there, Ralph. In there with guns. Lots of guns.'

'Ya talking like ya drunk, Philo.' Ford chortled. 'I asked ya who was shooting and all ya come up with is gibberish.'

The preacher moved closer to the sweat-soaked man and looked up into his unshaven features. 'The mayor went over there to try and find out what those evil horsemen want in Mohawk Flats.'

Ford glanced at the saloon at the five sweat-sodden animals tied up before it. 'Tom went in there?'

'Yep. And then there was another shot,' Tewksbury added. 'I think he's dead, Ralph. I think they've slain him.'

Still gripping the long handle of his hammer the huge man gritted his teeth and pondered the information he had just been given. His eyes flashed from the saloon to the man before him.

'Gunmen?'

'Five,' the preacher said.

Ford looked at the people who were hiding in the lanes which cut up from Main Street. 'Ain't none of ya yella bastards gone to see if Tom's OK?'

There was a mutual silence.

108

'Don't curse, Ralph,' Tewksbury ordered.

Enraged, the blacksmith leaned over and glared into the pious face of the preacher. 'Don't ya go trying to bully me, ya damn hypocrite. I ain't one of ya mindless sheep. I don't take orders from no sweet smelling little bastard like you, Philo.'

Tewksbury gasped and then was flung aside by a massive hand as the blacksmith moved to where he could see the faces of men hiding behind their women's petticoats. He aimed a large hand and powerful accusing finger at them.

'Now listen up and listen good,' Ford bellowed at them. 'I want ya all to go round town and try to find as many guns as there is to be found in this damn outhouse of a town. We gotta give them as good as they give us. Teach 'em it don't pay to mess with us no matter how many guns they got.'

A half-hearted murmur filled his ears.

'Tom might be lying in there dead or wounded bad.' Ford was furious with the so-called men he stared at. 'Just coz a bunch of gun-toting varmints ride in here killing, it don't follow that we gotta let them kill us. Does it?'

The men all made a pathetic noise which barely sounded like an agreement with the huge figure.

'Now go find as many guns as ya can,' Ford demanded. 'Dig out every damn weapon. Anything that'll stop them gunslingers before they decide to kill us all.'

109

The men vanished in accordance with the black-smith's demands.

Ford felt the bony fingers of the preacher's left hand clawing on his bare muscular forearm. He looked down at the thin Tewksbury as though studying an annoying mosquito – a mosquito he was about to swat.

'What, Philo?'

The preacher was wide eyed. 'How dare you bring my people down to the level of those animals.'

'They ain't your people, Preacher.' Ford corrected. 'You don't own them. They just happen to be folks who ain't used to dealing with heavily armed vermin.'

'Vengeance is mine said the Lord,' Tewksbury blurted. 'Not ours. His. This is a test. We must not wallow in the filth created by the Devil. We must be above such things. The Lord will deliver us.'

'Deliver us to Boot Hill,' The blacksmith snapped.

'Blasphemy.'

Ford returned his eyes to the saloon. 'If they done killed Tom I'll kill them all myself, Philo.'

'You'll burn in Hell.'

'Reckon so,' Ford snorted. 'I'm sure dressed for it.'

Philo Tewksbury watched the massive man turn away and follow some of the men he had sent in search of weapons and then returned his eyes to the saloon. He clutched his Bible in both hands and stepped down from the boardwalk.

The preacher began to walk straight at the saloon.

Snub Parsons lashed the hefty reins down on to the backs of the two horse buckboard team as the outskirts of Mohawk Flats came into view. The powerful horses responded and began to pull at their harnesses as the guard steered them toward the house where he could see the cowboy's mount tied to a porch upright. Yet no sooner had the pair of sturdy horses increased their combined pace when suddenly Trask thundered through their wheel dust astride his tall stallion.

It was as though the buckboard was stationary.

The horse and its master were galloping at full speed away from the four wheeled vehicle and its gruesome cargo.

Parsons watched in bewildered awe as the gunfighter balanced in his stirrups and steered the long legged stallion down the sun baked road and into the beginnings of the remote town. It took a special kind of horseman to ride like that, Parsons reasoned from his high perch. A brave, single minded rider with total faith in the horse beneath him.

Anyone could sit on a saddle and hang on to

their reins. It took courage and skill however to stand upright atop a galloping stallion whilst virtually balancing on the width of your boot heels.

Then Snub Parsons noticed something which he had not seen before. He gasped in awe: Trask was wearing his legendary gunbelt with its pair of infamous Colts gleaming in their holsters.

As the guard began to rein his team in the closer he got to the doctor's house, he continued to stare at the horseman who was increasing the distance between them with every beat of his heart.

Unlike Parsons, Trask did not slow his mount.

The seasoned gunman rode past Doc Bunston's place and seemed to be encouraging old Smoke to find even greater pace.

As Parsons hauled back on the buckboard's long leathers and stopped outside the small wooden structure, he could no longer see the gunfighter.

Trask had vanished into the swirling dust.

TWELVE

The shadows were getting longer along the valley. Trask had barely reached the beginnings of Mohawk Flats's main street when he was faced by a score of troubled faces spread out before his snorting stallion. The gunfighter dragged rein, halted his powerful mount and stared at them one by one. These were men who seemed to have already given up all hope of salvation; they were like the walking dead. None of them seemed to know where they were actually heading apart from the fact that they were moving away from the middle of the town itself. The seasoned champion of the helpless watched as they silently entered houses in an almost vain search for weapons.

Trask steadied his horse, dropped back down on to his saddle and went to speak to them as they passed him. Yet each time he opened his mouth their glazed eyes appeared to look away. These were not men as he recognized men to be. These were the broken souls of people who had somehow lost their way. He had seen this before many times in his long life. For the first time since he had ridden into Mohawk Valley he knew why he had been guided here.

Trask tugged the brim of his hat down to shield his eyes from the sinking sun and looked toward the twisting bend in the street. There was an unholy silence about the part of the crooked street which as yet he could not see. He wrestled with his eager horse and thought about the men who looked as though they had lost what little manhood they had once had. It did not sit well with the horseman. Trask looked at the faces of the men once more. A cold shiver traced his spine.

Then, as he was about to spur on the gunfighter spotted the larger figure with the gleaming, fleshy arms headed straight at him. There was a difference about Ralph Ford which set him apart from all the others he trailed. This man carried a massive long handled hammer over his shoulder as though it weighed little more than a feather; there was life in his face. A burning rage Trask recognized and understood.

There was also fire in Ford's eyes as they stared at the horseman before him. A fire which was created by anger. Ford aimed his large boots straight at Trask as though he were about to

114

unleash his fury on the stranger.

Trask touched the brim of his hat. 'Howdy.'

'Who are ya?' Ford shouted from the pit of his guts and increased his pace toward the horse and rider. 'If ya belonging to them bastards back there I'm gonna kill ya.'

Trask steadied his nervous mount and raised a hand. 'Hold up there, friend. I ain't belonging to nobody. I come here to try and round up a bunch of killers. The varmints who robbed the stage and killed a couple of folks back on the road.'

'I'm reckoning that ya ain't no cowboy by the looks of that fancy shooting rig.' The blacksmith stopped in his tracks. He glared at the horseman and inhaled deeply as though attempting to calm himself down. Trask had never seen a chest expand quite as much as Ford's did and it troubled him. This was a creature who looked as though he could tear a man apart with his bare hands. Trask did not wish to test his theory.

'Easy, pard,' Trask whispered. 'I ain't what ya think I am.'

'Then who and what are ya, old timer?' Ford growled as though only half his brain actually believed the words he had just heard the veteran rider utter.

'They call me Trask.' The gunfighter replied.

'Trask?' Ford tilted his head and studied the horseman with even more curiosity.

Trask nodded and kept his skittish mount under control as the blacksmith moved closer. 'Yep.'

'I heard about you,' Ford said.

Again Trask nodded at the large man who gleamed in the late afternoon sun.

'Ain't you some kinda gunman?' Ford was now so close he could have dragged Trask from his saddle at any time he so desired. 'A hired gun?'

'Nope,' Trask argued. 'I don't hire out to anybody, friend. I never have and I never will. I just kinda try and help folks who need my help.'

The blacksmith did not fully understand. He reached out and held the bridle of Trask's mount. His strength kept the animal quite still.

'I heard tell that ya mighty fast with them guns,' Ford recalled aloud. 'Is that true or just hogwash, old timer?'

Trask grinned. 'Ain't hogwash. I always have been kinda fast with these Eagle-Butt Peace-makers, pard.'

'And ya helps folks that need help. Right?' Ford raised his bushy eyebrows and studied the horse-man hard. This did not look like any knight in shining armour he had ever heard about. This was an old man.

'Yep,' Trask agreed.

'Why?' The muscular figure queried. 'Ain't no profit in that kinda work.'

'Maybe I'm just simple.'

Ralph Ford gave out a belly laugh. 'Then ya sure come to the right place, Trask. We sure do need a whole wagon load of help from somebody.'

'What are all these men doing?' Trask asked gesturing to the town's menfolk who were still wandering around like chickens that had just had their heads chopped off.

'I up and told 'em to look for guns,' Ford replied shaking his head. 'They couldn't find their noses by the looks of it.'

Trask flicked the safety loops off his pair of famous guns and slowly pulled them from their holsters. He saw the eyes of the blacksmith widen as they gazed upon the beautifully crafted Colts.

'You must be Trask,' Ford gasped. 'I heard tales of them fancy guns of yours and by the looks of 'em, the stories ain't as tall as I figured they was. That's sure a real fine bit of metal working.'

After checking that both weapons were fully loaded, the gunfighter returned both guns to their holsters. 'I want to know where those killers are holed up, pard. The exact place ya last seen them.'

'The saloon.' Ford pointed. 'All of them are in there and by the sound of them shots a while back, they already killed a couple of folks.'

'Which saloon?'

'There is only one, Trask,' Ford shrugged. 'Ain't a whole lotta men in Mohawk Flats that got the guts to defy their women and the preacher. Damn shame.'

THE MARK OF TRASK

Trask inhaled deeply. His guts still ached but he had no time to be troubled by it. There was a job to do, folks to help before the shooting started again. He gathered his reins and went to allow his horse to continue on when the blacksmith pulled on the bridle. Trask looked down at the face hard.

'What's troubling ya, big man?' Trask asked.

'My name's Ralph. Ralph Ford and I reckon I can help ya if'n ya want the help of a blacksmith.' Ford watched the reaction of the horseman.

Trask smiled. 'You ain't even got a gun, Ralph. Them varmints in the saloon are deadly gunmen. They'll kill anyone that gets in their way. They kill just for the pleasure of it.'

Ford raised the mighty hammer up. 'I don't need no guns. I got me this little toothpick, Trask. I can stove in a whole building with this damn thing.'

Trask raised an eyebrow. 'Yeah?'

'Yep.' Ford nodded.

Something was brewing inside Trask's imagination. He smiled and nodded. 'I just had me an idea, Ralph. Maybe I do need the help of a very large man with a very large toothpick.'

Ford grunted. 'Damn right ya do.'

There are many forms of courage. One of the rarest is when a man of faith uses his Bible as if it were a shield. Philo Tewksbury had as many enemies as friends in the town of Mohawk Flats but any of those who watched him as he walked toward the saloon could not doubt his total belief in the power he had preached about for most of his adult life.

But it was not just the townsfolk who witnessed the courageous man who recited the Lord's prayer with each stride of his thin legs as he crossed the wide street; it was also the deadly Largo gang. They too saw the preacher get closer and closer to the saloon.

Grant Largo led O'Mara and Tracy out on to the boardwalk and stared hard at the preacher.

Largo rested the knuckles of his left hand on his hip as his right hand stroked the wooden grip of his well notched holstered .45.

'Reckon ya ought to stop just about there, *amigo*,' Largo ordered the stick thin preacher.

Tewksbury stopped. 'The power of the Lord will destroy you if you do not cast away your weapons.'

Largo waved a hand at O'Mara. 'Git ya rifle, Snipe.'

The outlaw obeyed.

Largo returned his attention to the man standing thirty feet from him in the middle of the street. 'I figure on ya being the preacher of this town, stranger. Am I right?'

'That is correct, my son.' Tewksbury bowed his head slightly and brushed his lips across the cover of his Bible. 'Do ya heed my words?'

'Nope.' Largo answered quickly.

The preacher began to slowly continue his walk toward the substantial figure of Grant Largo. Still, his only protection was the Bible in his hands.

'I beg ya. The Lord begs ya. Stop this outrage now. The Lord shall forgive you, my son. Go now and seek forgiveness in ya prayers. We will allow you to leave town if you vow to implore forgiveness of the Almighty.'

Largo closed one eye. The other was aimed straight at the preacher. 'I told ya to stop, little man.'

'Repent,' Tewksbury insisted and he continued on toward the gunman.

Grant Largo stepped down from the boardwalk and strode to the thin man with more than his share of blind conviction. The outlaw stopped a mere couple of feet from the preacher and grabbed the Bible from Tewksbury's bony hands. He flicked its pages and nodded as though he could actually read. His eyes then rose and burned into Tewksbury like a pair of flaming daggers.

'Ya figure that this book can save ya, old timer?' the leader of the gang asked in a low drawl.

The preacher felt his throat go dry. 'Yes. The Lord shall protect me for I am pure.'

'Wrong.' Largo tossed the Bible over his shoulder and at the very same moment drew one of his guns. He squeezed its trigger after his thumb had pulled its hammer back until it had locked into position. The deafening blast was pointblank. A white flash of lethal venom spewed from the gun barrel. Smoke filled the gap between the pair. The bullet went straight into the middle of the preacher.

The town's womenfolk who were still sheltering across the wide street all shrieked in horror when they saw the massive hole appear in Tewksbury's back as the ball of lead made its exit of the thin torso. Gore was splattered a dozen yards behind the preacher across the almost yellow dusty street.

With blood trailing from the corners of his mouth Tewksbury closed his eyes. 'I forgive ya, my son.'

His words and their meaning were lost on the leader of the notorious gang. With total disdain Grant Largo turned on his heels and did not even bother to watch his victim crumple into the street behind him. The outlaw blew down the barrel of his .45 and then grinned at the faces of his watching men.

He stepped on the book and then twisted his boot until pages were torn from its middle.

'Now we gonna round us up some women, Grant?' Tracy asked his leader.

Largo reached to the closest of their horses and pulled a rope free of the saddle horn. He tossed it

121

to O'Mara. 'Round us up some womenfolk, Snipe. I got me a real powerful itch that gotta be scratched, boy.'

'Sure enough.' The outlaw made a loop and began to swing the rope above his head. He stepped over the body of the preacher and walked to where most of the best looking women were huddled. 'Any particular kind of female ya hankering for, Grant?'

Largo stepped up on to the boardwalk and turned to watch the outlaw. 'Nope. As long as they got a few teeth for me to knock out of their mouths, I'll be happy. Mighty happy.'

Keets staggered out of the saloon with a wry smile on his filthy face. 'I done found another box full of whiskey bottles, Grant.'

Largo nodded. 'Good enough. Killing that Bible puncher gave me a real powerful thirst.'

Pete Tracy stepped beside Largo. 'What about the bank? When we gonna relieve these folks of all their money?'

'Plenty of time for that afterwards, Pete.' Largo spat as his attention was drawn to the body of the preacher on the ground twenty feet from the edge of the hitching pole.

Tracy could not stop smiling at the thought of all the women they might get their hands upon. 'How many of these women we gonna service, Grant?'

Largo turned and pushed the swing doors apart.
'All of 'em.'

THIRTEEN

Blood stained the work clothes of the shotgun guard but little of it belonged to him. Most belonged to the dead and wounded he had brought to the very outskirts of town. Refusing to acknowledge his own exhaustion, Snub Parsons had carried both the wounded female passengers from the back of the borrowed buckboard into Doc Bunston's front parlour before he had climbed back up on to the high driver's board and whipped the two horse team into action once again.

The stagecoach guard had been instructed to take the pair of dead men's bodies to the undertaker at the other end of Mohawk Flats but knew that his ability to do so would depend on what was happening further into the remote settlement.

The sound of rattling harness chains filled the air as the sturdy horses obeyed the weary driver and ploughed on toward the heart of the remote town. Parsons lashed the reins down on to the backs of the lathered up horses as the vehicle negotiated the twisting streets and its tight corners. With screwed up eyes Parsons peered through the choking dust as the flatbed buckboard careened on toward the unknown destiny which awaited.

Like Trask before him, he too wondered where all the people were. Empty streets apart from a couple of stray dogs reinforced his anticipation of what lay ahead.

Where were all the people?

The question kept gnawing at his craw.

Where were they?

There did not seem to be another living soul to be found within the boundaries of the town. Street after street of nothing but dust. Parsons lashed the reins again and again. The team below his high vantage point powered on.

The sweat soaked guard leaned to his left, steered the galloping team around a corner and then saw the bewildering sight which had also stopped the seasoned gunfighter in his tracks only moments earlier. The bewildered townsmen were still vainly attempting to locate weapons with which they might be able to defend themselves against the Largo gang.

Suddenly Parsons appeared to have located at least some of the missing residents of the town. So many men that they were blocking his path.

Parsons dragged back on the weighty reins and then pushed his right boot against the brake pole. The buckboard came to a sudden halt. The brakes squealed. Dust drifted over Parsons and yet not one of the men who were blocking the street even seemed to notice his presence or the imminent danger.

'Are ya all loco?' Parsons shouted at them. 'I could have run ya all down.'

There were no answers.

No response.

It was as though they were all sleep walking in a vain bid to escape their nightmares.

The mystified stagecoach guard looped and secured the reins around the brake pole, grabbed his scattergun and then dropped down to the street before rubbing his neck.

He was confused and it showed in his dust-caked face.

Parsons tried to speak to several of the terrified people but their answers made little sense to him. All he did fathom from their mutterings was that they were seeking guns. But in Mohawk Flats to find a weapon of any description was like locating a waterhole in a desert.

Parsons walked away from them further along the street. Then to his surprise he spotted the one man in Mohawk Flats that he recognized.

'Trask,' Parsons murmured.

But Trask did not hear.

The veteran gunfighter was fifty yards away and slowly heading down into the heart of the town atride his chestnut stallion. Just as the guard went to call out he saw Trask swing his reins and crack them at the ground. The tall horse responded and raced around a corner.

A corner which Parsons knew only too well led right into main street. A thoroughfare he had travelled countless times during his career as a stagecoach guard.

'Damn it all,' Parsons cursed fearing for the safety of the famed Trask. 'Can't ya wait for a little help, old man?'

Snub Parsons looked back at the buckboard and then returned his attention to the lingering dust hanging in the dry air. Dust which was the only sign that Trask's horse had even been there at all. Uncertain as to what the smartest move might be, Parsons gripped his shotgun in his hands and swallowed hard. He had two choices.

He could drive the buckboard and its pitiful cargo after Trask straight to where the outlaws were waiting or he could remain on foot and use the scattergun more freely. Either option was probably a sure way to get yourself killed, his weary mind kept telling him, but for some strange reason Parsons was unafraid.

127

'Ya gotta help Trask, Snub, boy,' the guard told himself. 'If ya ever gonna amount to anything, ya gotta help that stubborn critter before he gets himself well and truly killed.'

With grim determination fuelling his resolve, Parsons cocked both hammers of the scattergun and started to run toward the dust in pursuit of the famed protector of the weak.

Hours earlier Trask had told the far younger stagecoach guard that he was a brave man. Snub Parsons did not realize it but he was about to prove that Trask was right.

FOURTEEN

Just as the chestnut stallion rounded a green wall of tangled bushes which clung to the trunk of an ancient oak, the rider realized that he had at last reached his destination. Death dwelled along main street. Trask could see the body of the preacher stretched out on the parched road close to the five tethered outlaw horses. He had also seen the last of the roped women being dragged screaming into the saloon by two of the deadly outlaws. The stallion continued on around the bend along main street. The shadows were getting longer, blacker, as the blazing sun made its way down toward the tree-covered mountain beyond the small settlement.

Trask steered the stallion into the darkest of the shadows on the same side of the street as the saloon a hundred yards ahead. He then leaned back, dug his boots into his stirrups and slowed his powerful mount with gloved hands. His reins were touching his chest by the time Trask managed to halt the eager horse beneath his saddle. Not pausing for even the beat of his heart he swung his right leg back and then dropped to the ground. The seasoned gunfighter led his prized stallion into an alley and quickly secured his reins to a porch upright. Trask thought about the black-smith he had sent around the array of buildings a few minutes before he had ridden away from the crowd of mindless men.

The gunfighter wondered how long it would take the burly Ford to reach the back of the saloon and do what they had agreed the muscular man with the hefty hammer would do.

All Trask needed was a diversion which would allow his old legs to get him into a position where he might be able to use his famed weaponry. He had total faith in his guns but he doubted his own body. He still hurt deep inside his guts, it felt as if he had already taken lead. Trask pressed the palm of his left hand against his shirt front and walked through the shadows back toward the bright sunlight which stretched the length of the main street.

No sooner had Trask reappeared in the street when scores of hysterical women and children raced passed him. They had been the lucky ones who had avoided the depraved outlaws ropes and the round-up. Trask paused and then buckled as a crippling pain in his middle tore through his resolve. He staggered. His left hand found a hitching pole and he steadied himself until the agony also passed.

He shook his head. Droplets of sweat defeated the band of his Stetson and fell from his temple. He breathed heavily and kept on forcing himself to think of the women he had to try and save from the creatures he sought. A vision of the handsome woman called Martha Stewart filled his mind. He had been too late to help her but he knew that he could save those who had been dragged into the distant drinking hole. He turned. His eyes screwed up and focused on the body lying on the ground surrounded by its own gore. He forced himself upright.

Trask removed his gloves and cast them aside. He staggered to a trough, scooped some of its water up and splashed it over his face. He could hear the cries for help starting. A burning anger filled his heart. He clenched his fists.

'Just one more time, Lord,' he said to himself as he managed to straighten up to his full height. 'One more time. Just one more time.'

The gunfighter went to walk when he heard his name being spoken in hushed tones coming from behind him. Trask paused and tilted his head until he was able to see the familiar figure of the stagecoach guard.

'Trask.' The voice of Snub Parsons filled the

veteran gunman's ears. The gunfighting legend slowly turned and looked at the guard with his scattergun clutched firmly in his hands. 'Ya ain't gonna take them varmints on without me. Ya hear? I'm in this to the end.'

Filling his lungs with air Trask patted the younger man on the shoulder. 'I hear ya, pard.'

Snub Parsons watched as Trask's hands slowly lowered until they were next to the holsters and the pear-handled, engraved ivory gun grips.

'Are them guns really magic, Trask?' Parsons innocently asked. 'Are they?'

Trask smiled. 'Only a fool would think that, Snub. Maybe that's why I reckon they are.'

Again both men's attention was drawn to the screams coming from the saloon. The guard looked into the emotionless face of the gunfighter. It showed no hint of the pain which now ravaged his every moment.

'What we gonna do, Trask?' Parsons asked as he stood shoulder to shoulder with the man who stared along the shadowy boardwalks toward the saloon. A saloon where the pitiful cries of women grew more and more intense.

Trask gritted his teeth thoughtfully. 'I'm gonna try and get them outlaws to come on out into the street, Snub.'

'How ya figuring on doing that?'

Trask gave a sigh. 'You'll see, pard. You'll see.'

Keets and Tracy had joined in the round-up of women. Their ropes had flown through the late afternoon air and encircled more than a quarter of their screaming prey easily. The few men that had remained in defiance of Ralph Ford's instructions had evaporated as soon as they had set eyes upon the heavily armed outlaws. None of them wanted to join the preacher on his way to the pearly gates.

What Trask had briefly witnessed as he had ridden into main street was now inside the evil smelling saloon. The cocktail of cigar smoke, sweat, blood and other bodily fluids now mixed together in the nostrils of every one of the occupants of the weathered structure.

Grant Largo stood like a merciless monarch from ancient times upon the top of the bar counter watching his men drag in their handsome catch like fishermen hauling in their nets. With a cigar smouldering in his teeth the leader of the gang marched up and down the top of the mahogany bar kicking stray glasses in all directions as he surveyed their spoils with eager eyes. The Largo gang had tasted the power their weaponry could give them before but none of them had ever experienced anything like this. A town which was virtually unarmed offered no defence to ruthless killers.

The peace loving people of Mohawk Flats were the victims of their own ideals; their innocence had been their downfall, for determined rats can can always find a way of infiltrating even the most pure of places. No heavenly palace is beyond the reach of vermin from the sewers of hell.

Inside the saloon the noise was becoming deafening. Pleads for mercy fell on deaf ears. The women's shrieks of fear and pain were challenged only by the rampant laughter of the outlaws as they satisfied themselves on their captured bounty.

Encrusted in his own gore, Tom Jacobs had sat helplessly in the chair he had been placed upon minutes earlier. Minutes which had felt like an eternity to the wounded man who had already seen at least a quarter of his blood spill out on to the sawdust covered floorboards.

Blood still crept from the brutal bullet wound in his thigh but now he had other things on his dazed mind.

Revenge.

It was a word which was totally alien to the previously harmless man. But it was becoming the only word which managed to fill his befuddled brain.

Revenge. He had heard the shot which had ended Tewksbury's life and knew that if a man of God could end up that way then it looked pretty grim for the rest of the townsfolk. He had to do something. Something which only hours earlier he would have never even considered. Tom Jacobs had to try and destroy those who were hellbent on destroying everything he and the rest of Mohawk Flats stood for.

Revenge was a bitter word but Jacobs was more than willing to risk whatever moments of existence he had remaining to achieve that goal. Kill or be killed. Do nothing and still end up six feet under was a futile alternative.

The mayor was not secured in the chair. The outlaws had reasoned that being so badly wounded their unarmed prisoner could do little if anything to them.

Jacobs was going to try and prove them wrong. He glanced at the women. Some were little more than children whilst others were old but they were all the same to these cruel men. Jacobs shuddered. These were the women of his town. Some if not most of them were related to him in some way or another and he felt responsible for their plight.

Some screamed out to Jacobs for help and yet he could not do anything. Not against such overwhelming odds. Or could he? The mayor lowered his head in shame and stared at the crimson sawdust at his feet and desperately tried to think of a way of helping them.

Then out of the corner of his eye he saw the only one of the gang who was not participating in the carnal round-up. Vance Largo was asleep with his head resting on his wrists at the table five feet from where the mayor was sitting. Jacobs tilted his head and glanced at the four other heavily armed men. They had nothing on their minds except one thing.

The one thing which could be their downfall, he thought. No man ever thought rationally when indulging in the most basic of desires, not even heavily armed outlaws. Once the sap was rising there was nothing any man could do but ride that bucking mustang until you reached the end of the trail.

A new resolve filled the mayor.

Jacobs looked back at the grips of Vance's holstered guns; guns the young outlaw had wanted to use on him before the whiskey had taken its toll.

The mayor licked his dry lips.

If he could just get to those guns he could drag them from their holsters and open up on the vermin who were violating the town's womenfolk. Jacobs managed to make the hardback chair move a couple of inches across the sawdust. His eyes darted up and looked at the four other outlaws. They were totally unaware of his existence at this moment in time.

They had all forgotten about him.

Gripping the arms of the chair, Jacobs lifted his weight off the seat of the chair, wiggled his rear and managed to make the chair move another few inches toward the table. Again his eyes looked up.

Again they had not even noticed.

The mayor kept on repeating his actions until he was sitting within two feet away from where Vance Largo snored. His heart was pounding inside his chest.

He had to remain calm, he told himself.

Jacobs kept his head slightly lowered but was able to look up through his limp hair at the men as they began their assault on the women.

Suddenly a fury welled up inside the mayor. It was something he had never experienced before not even when Keets had sent a well aimed bullet through his leg. Jacobs rubbed the sweat from his face and then ran his damp fingers through his hair as he straightened up on his chair.

Still none of them even saw him.

He was invisible for the gang members had something far more appetizing to feast their attention and hands upon, there had to be twenty or more women of various ages held by three cutting ropes in the middle of the saloon.

The mayor watched as Keets tore the clothing from one of the youngest of the females as he searched for flesh. Then Grant Largo dragged one of the plumpest of the screaming women from the restraints of the rope and hoisted her off her feet and up on to the bar counter. There was no subtlety in Largo's actions. He slapped the woman until her eyes rolled up under her eyelashes and then grabbed at her high necked dress front. His strong fingers clawed at the fabric until he was able to rip it down to her navel.

Then men roared with laughter as the females cried out in fear and humiliation.

Jacobs clenched his fists in rage. He glanced at the closest of the gun grips poking out from Vance Largo's holster. Without even thinking of what he was undertaking, the mayor of Mohawk Flats grabbed the weapon and dragged it clear of its leather constraints. The snoring outlaw had not felt a thing. Jacobs held the gun on the blind side of the outlaws as he manoeuvred the chair around to the other side of the table. Reaching his goal the wounded man removed the other gun from its holster.

Two guns.

Twelve bullets.

Was that enough?

Jacobs was panting like an exhausted hound. The guns in his hands were hidden from the other men's view by the card table. As the outlaws became more boisterous and noisy he cocked both guns.

They did not hear it.

His eyes narrowed as he watched the four killers. He wanted to kill them all but he had never even held a six-shooter before let alone fire one. A thousand doubts began to fill his blood-starved brain.

What if he fired the guns but ended up hitting some of the women? The outlaws had them all roped so close together that it would take a damn good shot not to hit one of the innocent women, he mused.

What if he miraculously did manage to hit one or more of the outlaws but fail to kill them?

What would they in turn do to the women?

Revenge worked both ways.

Jacobs had heard that there was nothing more dangerous than a wounded animal and these men were little more than two legged animals. They might slaughter the women inside the saloon and then go hunting for fresh game.

His head dropped until his chin touched his shirt collar. He stared at the guns in his hands.

What should he do?

What could he do?

The loss of so much blood had drained not only his stamina but also his ability to concentrate. Jacobs tried not to listen to the pitiful screams. He tried not to watch but his eyes strayed to where the four depraved outlaws were feeding their brutal desires. Grant Largo had found the woman's flesh he so feverishly craved for up on top of the counter. To the blurred eyes of the mayor it was as though he were watching a cowboy riding a bucking bronco.

Jacobs knew he had no chance against even drunken gunslingers like these but he had to try and stop them. Stop them before they left their evil seeds in all of the town's womenfolk.

A chilling thought swept over the mayor. He imagined the spawn of such depraved creatures walking the town's streets. Jacobs knew that he had little time to prevent that sickening occurrence. He had to act and act now.

Somehow he managed to struggle free of the chair and raised himself up until he was standing. He raised the guns in his shaking hands and tried to aim but his eyes would not see clearly any longer.

Maybe he could bluff them into submission, he reasoned. Would they be like the rest of the men in town and simply raise their hands when faced by guns?

It was worth a try.

'Stop or I'll kill ya,' Jacobs yelled out at the top of his lungs. 'Ya hear me? Stop or I'll surely kill the whole bunch of ya. Savvy?'

Grant Largo did not even pause his humiliation of the woman bent over before him as his hips kept crashing into her ample buttocks. Without any hint of fear the outlaw gang leader glanced across the wide saloon at the wounded Jacobs.

'Pete!' Largo snapped down at Tracy.

Pete Tracy swung the small herd of women he had held in check by the rope, squinted through the dusty beams of sunlight and then drew his gun, cocked its hammer and squeezed its trigger.

The ear splitting gunshot echoed within the walls of the saloon.

There was no reply.

FIFTEEN

The acrid aroma of gunsmoke lingered in the putrid air of the saloon as it continued to trail from the barrel of Pete Tracy's six-shooter. The startled faces of the captive females were etched with total disbelief. They had just witnessed the outlaw fire a single shot at their mayor. The bullet had carved its way through the throat of the already half dead Tom Jacobs and finished the valiant man off.

Jacobs lay on the floor beside the still snoring Vance Largo as his older brother threw the woman he had just satisfied himself with from the bar counter and went to grab for another.

Then without warning the rear wall and door of the saloon began to reverberate as the thunderous racket of the blacksmith's mighty hammer filled all of their ears. The wall shook; the door buckled. Following Trask's instructions to the letter, Ralph

Ford was smashing his hammer into the very fabric of the structure in a bid to distract the five outlaws. The huge man had the resolve and strength to turn the saloon into mere splinters should he have wished.

Pictures fell from their nails on the rear wall just beyond Jacob's prostrate body. Shattering glass from their frames flew up into the air catching the brilliant rays of the sun which snaked its width.

'What in tarnation is that, Grant?' Tracy drunkenly asked the man above him.

Stunned by the noise, Grant Largo released his grip on the young woman he was about to haul upward. The outlaw leapt down to the floor and stood fastening his pants studs.

'Some real dumb critter is dicing with death out back by the sounds of it, boys,' Largo boomed.

'Sounds like a real ornery buffalo to me.' O'Mara released his grip on his rope and all of the women he had contained fell to their knees. The outlaw who had earned his reputation as a sniper during the war rushed to the side of Largo. 'How many of them do ya figure there are?'

'Enough to kill,' Largo spat.

The noise increased.

The building's walls kept on shaking as though withstanding a tornado's venom. Ford continued his onslaught.

Largo tucked his shirt tails into his pants and

then drew one of his guns and cocked its hammer. He was about to speak when he caught sight of his still unconscious brother. 'Vance. Git up ya damn locobean.'

'I'll wake him.' Tracy dropped his rope and rushed to where Vance still snored and pulled the youngest of their gang to his feet. He slapped his face until his eyes partially opened.

Vance snarled at the man who kept on slapping his face and then both his hands went for his guns. A confused look filled the face of the drunken outlaw.

'Where's my guns?'

'There.' Tracy released his hold and then pointed down at the dead mayor who still held the weapons in his lifeless hands.

'How'd he git 'em?' Vance Largo staggered to the body and bent over. He pulled the six-shooters free and then straightened back up. 'And who killed him?'

'I did, Vance.' Pete Tracy trained his eyes on the rear door as it began to fracture under the constant bombardment of Ford's hefty hammer.

The youngest of the Largo brothers looked annoyed. 'Damn ya, Pete. I wanted to kill him.'

'Ya lucky he didn't kill you, Vance,' Tracy said from the corner of his mouth as the three other outlaws marched to where they were standing looking at the wall.

Vance Largo staggered to face his older sibling. 'How come ya let Pete kill that critter, brother Grant? Ya knew I wanted to do it.'

'Shut up,' Grant Largo growled anxiously.

'But—'

'Ya heard me, boy.' The eldest Largo grabbed the face of his brother and squeezed his mouth shut, pushing him to one side. 'This is serious.'

'Who'd ya figure that is, Grant?' Keets asked, as he cocked the hammers of both his guns and aimed them at the door, chunks of wood flying from its surface.

Grant Largo snarled. 'Whoever it is I reckon he oughta be eating lead, boys. Fire at that damn door and wall. I figure our bullets will cut right through that wood.'

'And kill the fool.' Tracy laughed.

'Then we can carry on sowing our oats.' O'Mara grinned.

Largo nodded. 'Damn right.'

Driven by their desire to continue their determined onslaught on the women the five outlaws readied their weapons and began to fire viciously at the back wall of the saloon. The sound was deafening and drowned out the hammering. The room filled with the choking gunsmoke from their hot barrels. They emptied more than fifty bullets into the door.

Then Grant Largo raised a hand.

They all stopped firing and began to reload.

A satisfied smirk etched the gang members' faces. The destructive hammering had stopped.

'Reckon we got the bastard?' Keets pondered as he holstered one weapon and started to reload the other.

'Sure we got him. The hammering's quit, ain't it?' Vance Largo said, before drunkenly staggering toward the shattered door still smoking with bullet holes which now graced its surface.

Grant Largo glanced at his brother. 'And where the hell are you headed, Vance, boy.'

The younger of the notorious brothers dropped one of his guns into its holster, grabbed hold of what remained of the door handle and turned it. 'I'm gonna see—'

The sentence was never completed. No sooner had Vance Largo pulled the door toward him when a blinding flash of buckshot roared like thunder out of the alley from Snub Parsons's deadly scattergun.

Vance Largo was knocked off his feet by the sheer force of the blast. He landed in a lifeless heap beside the body of Tom Jacobs.

O'Mara snapped the chamber of his reloaded gun shut and clawed back on its hammer. He went to fire when the second barrel of Parsons's scattergun erupted into blood-curdling action.

Grant Largo had felt some of the pellets pepper

his face before he had time to duck. He wiped the blood from his cheek and shouted at his remaining men.

'C'mon. Let's git out of here.'

'What about Vance and Snipe?' Tracy yelled before firing three shots through the open doorway.

'They're dead. C'mon,' Largo spat. With Tracy and Keets on his heels the outlaw leader turned and raced toward the cowering women close to the long bar counter.

Running backwards, Keets fired his fully loaded guns at the rear door. 'What ya doing, Grant? We oughta be headed out to the horses not going back to these womenfolk.'

'Ya ever heard about human shields, Keets?' Largo snorted as the three deadly outlaws reached the roped women. 'Ain't nobody gonna fire at us and risk hitting these gals with no buckshot.'

Each of the trio of desperados grabbed a rope and tightened them around their prisoners.

'Damn,' Tracy cursed as he hid behind his group of shrieking women. 'I'd never have thought of this, Grant.'

'That's why I'm the boss, Pete boy.' Largo kept one eye on the rear door as he began to push his half dozen captives toward the swing doors.

The outlaws grouped themselves together with the roped women surrounding their every step.

They moved slowly toward the swing doors with one hand on a rope and the other gripping a cocked six-shooter. The sunlight drew them like moths to a beckoning flame yet there was only retribution awaiting the three cowardly outlaws on the main street.

Their clothing was ripped and torn. Some were virtually naked but all of the town's women who had found themselves encircled by ropes knew that they were the lucky ones. Lucky to still be alive and not dead like Philo Tewksbury and Tom Jacobs. The screams had made way for whimpering.

What remained of the Largo gang moved between their bleeding and humiliated victims out on to the boardwalk to where the five horses were tied to the hitching rail. A dark shadow stretched along the saloon side of the long winding street but where the preacher lay beneath a blanket of flies the sun still burned down without mercy.

Now the outlaws had a problem: now they had to somehow get from the safety of the women and to their tethered mounts.

Pete Tracy was first to release his grip on his rope whilst nervously training one of his primed guns on the women held within its loop. The man who was an expert with explosives and always carried a satchel full of dynamite sticks in his saddle bags was visibly afraid. Somehow within a matter of seconds the tables had been turned and Tracy could not fathom how. The outlaw ducked under the hitching pole and pulled at his reins until they freed, all the time aiming the barrel of his gun at the women, closest to him, as though daring them to try and run away from the board-walk.

Grant Largo kept the women trapped in his lasso pulled close to him as he stooped and stared over their heads. His eyes darted up and down the street trying to adjust to the bright sunlit buildings opposite him and the black shadows he still stood in.

'Can ya see anyone, Pete?' Largo asked.

'Nobody at all,' Tracy replied. 'The street looks damn deserted to me, Grant.'

'But is it?'

Keets kicked at his group of women as he herded them like a frustrated wrangler along the boardwalk until he reached the other end of the long hitching pole where his horse stood beside the others. He too kept searching the wide thor-oughfare for trouble whilst maintaining his grip on his shield of human flesh.

'Ya see anyone, Grant?' Keets shouted above the whimpering of the women.

Just like his two cohorts, Largo could not see any apparent threat in the main street. Sensing the jeopardy was still behind them and would come from the unseen man with the lethal scattergun, Largo manoeuvred the wall of sobbing women around until they faced the swing doors of the saloon. He backed away and stepped down into the street. He swung around in all directions gripping one of his smoking guns in his hand.

Then he heard a noise inside the saloon beyond the gunsmoke which still hung about four feet above the blood stained ground.

'That dirt-chewing varmint with the scattergun is in the saloon, boys,' Largo snarled fearfully. 'Reckon he ain't through just yet.'

'I'm for hightailing it, Grant.' Keets dropped the rope holding the five women he had managed to rustle up earlier.

The women somehow managed to free themselves from its rough constraint and scattered. Even the oldest of them managed to run for cover. Keets slipped under the reins of the horses and gave his leathers a tug. 'I'm for mounting and riding, boys. What ya say?'

Largo knew that the only reason the buckshot had not sought any of them out was because they still had plenty of the womenfolk guarding their hides. The outlaw leader wanted to step into his stirrup and ride as Keets was urging, but knew that once he was on top of his high shouldered mount he was an easy target for anyone with the grit to try their luck.

For the first time in a long while he was indecisive and more than a little fearful.

Tracy was becoming more and more nervous.

'Tell us what to do, Grant,' he implored his leader. 'We gonna ride or we gonna go back in that saloon and finish off that shotgun toting bastard? What'll it be?'

'What we doing? Riding or fighting?' Keets shouted out from between the horses. 'Grant?'

'I could toss a few sticks of dynamite around,' Tracy suggested. 'That might buy us some time and give us cover. Ya figure I should?'

Grant Largo did not have time to answer the mind crippling questions. He was glued to the ground as his eyes saw something he could not have ever conceived in his wildest imaginings. A defiant, tall figure walked out of the shadows and then stopped in the blazing rays of the setting sun. Trask slowly turned to face them.

The sun was on his back.

'Free them women,' Trask called out as his hands hovered above his gun grips.

There was a hundred feet between the gunfighter and the three outlaws, who still had nearly a dozen women protecting them.

'Who is that, Grant?' Keets asked, as he stared from over his saddle from the protection of the motionless horses.

Largo squinted at the man with the sun on his

back. 'I ain't set eyes on that critter before.'

'Oh no.' Pete Tracy felt as though someone had just snapped his spine into fragments. He recognized the tall man standing in weathered trail clothes. 'Not him.'

Largo looked back for a fraction of a heartbeat at Tracy.

'What ya say, Pete? Why ya sounding so feared?'

Tracy was shaking. 'T-that's Trask.'

Largo heard the name and screwed up his eyes and tried to focus upon the man who had squared up to them. A man who held his hands just above the grips of his holstered seven inch barrelled Eagle-Butt Peacemakers.

'Trask?' Largo repeated the name. 'Are ya sure? That critter is old. Darn old.'

Suddenly there was another noise inside the saloon. Snub Parsons was moving through the room toward them. As the three outlaws turned their attention on the saloon, Parsons fired one of his shotgun barrels at the window furthest away from where the women were standing.

'What the hell?' Largo yelled out.

A million splinters of shattering glass cascaded from the window frame; buckshot spewed out into the street. Parsons threw himself on to the saloon floor and blasted his hefty weapon again. Like a swarm of crazed hornets the small balls of buckshot flew before Largo.

Desperately, Keets fanned his gun hammer wildly and sent bullets into the dark belly of the saloon. One of their horses reared up and then crashed forward through the weathered hitching pole. It bucked and then leapt over the outlaw and raced away from the saloon.

In the deafening confusion the captive women finally had their chance to escape. They scattered in all directions leaving their captors standing by the four remaining horses.

Pete Tracy had had enough.

'You can stay here and git shot but I'm for getting out of here right now.' Tracy grabbed his saddle horn, wheeled up on to his mount and turned the animal away from the mayhem.

'Get ready to die,' Trask announced and began to slowly walk toward the men outside the saloon.

'I don't care who ya are, old timer.' Largo hastily reloaded his guns as his eyes remained glued on the figure who defiantly approached them. Snapping both his guns' chambers shut, he gripped his weapons in his sweating hands and stepped closer to his horse. 'I'm gonna kill ya.'

After emptying his guns into the saloon the terrified Tracy hauled his reins hard to his right, spurred and started to urge his mount away from the gunsmoke.

'Git back here, ya yella belly,' Largo shouted at the rider. Keets had managed to find enough bullets in his belt to load one of his guns. 'What ya figure we oughta do, Grant?'

'Kill that old timer, Keets,' Largo ordered. 'What else?'

Both gunmen standing beside their horses raised their guns and squeezed their triggers.

Faster than either of the hardened outlaws had ever seen anyone draw before, Trask's hands hauled his guns from their holsters and returned fire.

Three of Trask's bullets hit Grant Largo dead centre. He was knocked off his feet and fell beneath his horse's hoofs. Keets lasted a little longer as he leapt on to the ground and continued to fire.

With bullets passing to either side of him, fearlessly Trask kept on walking and firing at the man who lay on his belly. Then his bullets found their mark. He saw Keets's head take shots from both his guns.

It exploded.

Trask stopped and looked at the horseman and raised one of his Peacemakers.

He fired. His bullet found the saddle-bags filled with dynamite. The explosion shook the entire town. There was little left apart from a crater surrounded by smouldering flesh when the smoke lifted.

Snub Parsons ran from the saloon to where

Trask was standing and looked around at the bloody evidence of the showdown. Just like the legendary gunfighter, he felt no sense of satisfaction from their handiwork. The massive blacksmith appeared from the side of the saloon with his long handled hammer resting on his shoulder.

'Is it over?' Ralph Ford asked.

'Yep.' Trask holstered his guns, rubbed his guts and then turned away from the carnage. 'It's over.'

'Trask?' Parsons piped up. 'Where ya going?'

Trask looked over his shoulder. He pointed at the hitching rail. 'Git one of them dead men's horses and I'll show ya, pard.'

FINALE

The two horsemen had negotiated the meandering trail which led up through the tree-covered mountain far above the valley and the remote community of Mohawk Flats in less than an hour. The riders had not spoken since they had started out after the brutal bloodbath. Trask sat astride his tall stallion and led the way whilst Snub Parsons followed on one of the dead outlaws' sturdy mounts. The closer they got to the summit the more Parsons had noticed his companion slumping over the neck of his faithful mount.

It was obvious that Trask was in pain.

Agonizing pain.

As the trail widened to reveal the sight of a million trees far below their high vantage point, Trask drew rein and then slowly dismounted. Parsons eased himself off the unfamiliar saddle and stared at the man he secretly regarded as his hero.

The younger man sensed that there was something wrong with his companion – something very wrong. Snub Parsons watched as the famed gunfighter stroked the neck of his tall stallion and gave the hand tooled gunbelt hanging across Smoke's neck a wry smile.

'How come we stopped here, Trask?' Parsons asked.

Trask did not reply. He walked unsteadily away from his horse to a grassy rise and then eased himself down until he was seated with his back against a tree trunk opposite the impressive view.

With weary eyes Trask stared at the sinking sun, knowing it would be the last sunset he would ever see. Yet there was no anger in the frail figure he had become. Only a look of relief that at long last he could rest.

Parsons moved to the neck of the stallion and also looked in awe at the gunbelt branded with the name of 'Trask' upon its leatherwork. He then glanced at the seated man who seemed to have aged on the ride up to the top of the mountain.

'Ya look kinda ill, Trask.'

Trask looked at the young man and corrected him. 'I ain't ill, pard. I'm dying.'

'Were ya shot back there?' The guard could not conceal his genuine concern. 'I didn't see no blood.'

Trask shook his head gently. 'Nope, none of

157

their bullets even come close.'

'Then what's wrong?' There was urgency and panic in the younger man's trembling voice. 'How can ya be dying?'

'My ride is over, Snub,' Trask uttered as he looked out at the setting sun, which was making the sky turn red. 'I figure I'll just sit here and wait for some angel to take pity on this old carcass. Don't bury me – I'll be just fine.'

There was confusion in Parson's mind and heart. 'If ya was ill how come ya didn't go to old Doc Bunston? He's a darn good sorebones. He'd have saved ya.'

Trask closed his eyes and leaned back. 'There ain't nothing he could have done, pard. I've known for quite a while that my day's were numbered. My sand has just run out, that's all. There ain't no call to fret none. Where I'm headed there ain't no more pain. I'm kinda tuckered fighting the pain.'

Parsons knelt beside the man he felt as though he had known all his days and not the mere handful of hours since they had encountered one another. 'Trask?'

'I ain't Trask, boy.' The older man sighed. 'Never was. Folks just tagged me with the name when I bought them guns. Reckon it's coz the name was branded on the belt. It just stuck.'

Snub Parsons was bewildered. 'Then who was

the real Trask?'

'It don't matter none,' Trask smiled. 'I figured that you might want to be Trask. A new Trask just like I used to be before I got old.'

'I don't understand.'

Trask pointed at his horse and the belt hanging over its neck. 'When I'm through I want ya to take old Smoke and them guns, boy. Ya proved ya worth back there. I reckon you'll be a mighty fine Trask.'

Parsons went to speak when he saw the agony in the face of the sick man. Even the fading light could not hide it from his knowing eyes.

'I'll be Trask?'

Again Trask nodded. 'If'n ya want to be.'

'But I ain't no gunfighter.' Parsons admitted. 'How can I ever match your skill with them shooting irons?'

Trask looked upon his prodigy. 'The guns will protect ya, Snub, boy. They'll never let ya down. Trust them but never use them for nothing but good. Promise me that.'

Parsons felt a lump in his throat, 'I-I promise.'

Trask closed his eyes again. A tear rolled from one of them and dripped upon the sleeve of the confused Parsons. He watched as the red glowing rays of light faded from the tortured features.

A final sigh murmured from the lips of the old gunfighter. His head rolled to the side. He was gone.

Parsons stood and looked down at the body of the frail man and then his eyes went to the guns.

The guns of Trask.

'Trask is dead. Long live Trask.' He whispered and looked up at the sky and the thousands of stars which had appeared without him even noticing, '*Adios,* pard. Ya got my solemn word I'll not let ya down.'